The Silence and Beyond

A work of fiction
by

M. L. Schubert

DENVER, COLORADO

The Silence and Beyond is a work of fiction. Names, characters, places, and incidents are the products of the author's imagination or are used fictitiously. Any resemblance to actual events or persons, living or dead, is entirely coincidental.. The opinions expressed in this manuscript are solely the opinions of the author and do not represent the opinions or thoughts of the publisher. The author has represented and warranted full ownership and/or legal right to publish all the materials in this book.

The Silence and Beyond
The story of a girl-genius and her only true friend
All Rights Reserved.
Copyright © 2014 M. L. Schubert
v3.0

Cover Photo © 2014 JupiterImages Corporation. All rights reserved - used with permission.

All rights reserved, including rights to reproduce this book or portions thereof in any form whatsoever without permission in writing from the author except by a reviewer who may quote brief passages to print in a magazine or newspaper.

Outskirts Press, Inc.
http://www.outskirtspress.com

ISBN: 978-1-4787-2134-5

Outskirts Press and the "OP" logo are trademarks belonging to Outskirts Press, Inc.

PRINTED IN THE UNITED STATES OF AMERICA

In Memory of
Those I Have Loved and Lost

*"At the crossroads I covered my ears with frost
and wept for what I had lost"*

Hannah Senesh

We must talk of them all,
the roots and the stems of us,
flowers that have fallen,
leaves and branches reaching out
into a storm of winters like this
and all the rest of the seasoned
bittersweetness of being
buried beneath our words,
our longings, our terrible eyes
that will not rest from what
we have ever seen
in Jerusalem flowers,
the bloody red,
the yellow stars of us,
the brilliant blue.

Prelude

I keep thinking about Bethie's death, which now has become an endless dialogue with the awesome responsibility we share in each other's lives. So much to remember, so much I hadn't understood-- the mysteries inside our complicated friendship, the long silences between us, and then, after she died, how her story became our story, Bethie's and mine, flowing together into a stream of endings and beginnings.

PART I

"Roots and Stems of Us"

ONE

V an Gogh has been quoted as saying that a friend's suicide turns friends into murderers. If Vincent had it right, if the neglect of a loved one can contribute in even a small measure to a final act of desperation, then on April 23, 1974, I became a murderer.

When Bethie's last letter to me arrived, we were living in Irvine, and I was slowly drowning in a stream of marital, parenting and household needs. These continual demands and promises of my time seemed endless until her letter came with the force of both an end and a beginning crashing into the same instant and changing my life forever.

Earlier that morning: As always, I'm fixing Mark's breakfast while we listen to the news on the radio.

"No news of any import," he decides and turns down the volume, then drinks his coffee and starts on his usual toast and eggs while I cut up vegetables for the stew that will be slow-cooking all day in our chubby, red Crock-Pot.

After pouring himself a second cup, "Carol, sweetheart," Mark summons, "I need you to help me edit my new script tonight. Let's get started right after dinner."

"What about dishes and bedtime stories? I wanted..."

"Leave the dishes until morning, okay?"

"What about three bedtime regimes...baths, stories, and little Judd...he still needs a bottle."

"Carol, you baby him too much."

"He's still a baby," I remind him while feeling my stomach tighten in its carefully exercised way of holding back anger, warning me I could easily lose valuable parts of my life if I let go.

"Just cut things short tonight," Mark insists. "You know, like when we had more time for ourselves." He reaches out and pulls me away from the stove and onto his lap. "You look so pretty in that little apron." He runs his fingers through my long black curls and tickles my ear with his lips.

"Hey...what's this now, Mark? You've got to go, right?"

"Well, maybe we could..."

"Not now, Honeyman," I say, pulling on his tie.

"Why not?"

"You know we can't now."

"I guess not," he agrees and sets me back up on my feet. "Okay, then, tonight. First my script, then some fun." He gives me a long kiss, then goes for his jacket and briefcase.

After he leaves, I breathe a momentary sigh of relief, then hurry upstairs to wake Wendy and then Daniel, whose roommate, baby brother Judd, is standing at the side of his crib jumping up and down and gurgling something seeming meaningless but adorable, his signal that it's time for all of us to begin our day.

I'd signed up to work with my neighbor, Jenna, that Friday on the hot dog sale at our children's school. After that, it's my turn to take Daniel and his friend Scotty to soccer practice. Then I'll take Wendy to her piano lesson while, with any luck, little Judd will nap on the back seat and I'll crochet gifts for the Temple Emmanuel Holiday Bazaar while waiting for Wendy. And soon after that, we'll be going back to pick up Daniel where he'll be waiting for me at Scotty's home after soccer practice. My usual day. A little dull most of the time but predictable, and there's a kind of safety in that when raising children, although one remains always still vulnerable to the inevitable unexpected.

It's hard to separate the letter's impact from the rush of events that followed, but that April morning in 1974 is like a dream engraved with haunting clarity.

I'm walking out into the shade of our huge pine trees to the mailbox while feeling the comfort of my long hair falling over my shoulders and swinging gently against my cheeks. It's one of those glorious Southern California spring days. I notice the Natal Plums in the hedge and pick off one of the edible scarlet berries and suck in its milky juice, then carry in a few more for the children along with the mail.

Soon I'm sorting through the pile of mail and come upon a letter without a return address. I open it and scan down quickly to the signature. It's from Bethie, my closest friend in high school and college. I haven't seen or heard from her in over two years. She'd visited us in Irvine, and I still regret we argued, but I can't seem to recall now about what, only that I'd felt relieved when she left.

Folded behind the letter are worn copies of some poems I'd written to her during our years together at La Mesa High School, and there's also one she must have recently written, with the title "Last Sonnet." Puzzled, I set it aside and read the letter first:

> Dear Carol,
> I give you back your promise and poems no longer needed.
> Say goodbye to Wendy for me.
> Bethie

I read the last line again. *Say goodbye to Wendy for me.*

Why say goodbye to Wendy? Suddenly I realize her letter's terrible message. I grab the page with the poem and read it.

My Last Sonnet

They'll wear my bloody shoes when I am gone
Be weeping dressed to please each other's sight
Say what I do is madness or not right
They'll pity me and talk of me till dawn
Pretending some that once I held them dear,
And they were truly frightened though they smiled,
Will calculate me backwards to the child,
Say everything they think you ought to hear.
In the beginning were my seeds to end.
At last I'll break this cage and I'll be free.
But you, wet-eyed philosopher of me,
You'll go lonely-shouldered, still my friend,
Remembering who you loved when she was bold,
The girl who knew she never would grow old.

I rush to the phone while hearing the scream inside my head begging Bethie not to say goodbye to Wendy, and then immediately realize I can't call her since I don't have her current phone number. She'd mentioned moving to teach at some university the following fall, and I don't remember which one. Moreover, I admit to myself that I purposely lost track of her whereabouts because of the argument between us during her visit. That cutting truth fills me now with shame.

After a frantic search, I find an old list of phone numbers and dial her mother's home in Tucson, hoping she'll be able to give me Bethie's current phone number. Now nearly hysterical, I try to get through to the person who answers on the other end of the line.

"Hello, please... Hello!" Muffled sounds. "Hello, is this Mrs. Hartung?"

"She isn't able to come to the phone now. This is her sister Marilyn."

"This is Carol Simon, a friend of Bethie's. I'm trying to get in touch with her, but I've misplaced her phone number."

"Is this you, Carol? Carol Mandell?"

"Yes." I'm relieved she remembers me. "I need to get in touch with Bethie and I'm wondering if Mrs. Hartung has her phone number."

A pause, then, "Bethie is...she's dead, Carol."

Her words seep in, connecting my brain to the loss of any hope.

We're both crying now, but I somehow manage to ask her, "How did Bethie die?"

"Pills. We were told she took a lot of them."

When she mentions the funeral, I say that I'll plan to come. She tells me it's to be on Sunday at Greenacres Cemetery, and adds, "But it's to be a private ceremony for family only." Then, in helpless silence, I hear her say, "I'm sorry, Carol, but it's what Bethie's mother wants."

I sit by the phone for a long time, very slowly letting Bethie's death click into the place in my mind I'd always left open for it, the first time she'd announced proudly as we walked the halls of La Mesa High together, "I'm never going to get old."

Once she even ran out in front of a line of cars and I pulled her back. She then tried to reassure me with her theories of predetermined fate.

"It isn't my time yet," she insisted.

"Well, they don't know that," I reminded her. She laughed and, pulling at a strand of my hair, teased saying, "You're quite clever, Carol, I hope you know."

I'm never going to grow old, her voice echoes as I turn and look out of the front windows. A view of flowers of every color on the hilly divisions of our lawn spreads before me. Flowers that seemed vibrant that morning now look dull, stillborn. Even the yellow, open daffodils. I try to visualize exactly how Bethie looked the last time I saw her, how she wore her hair, what outfit she had on when she left our house in Irvine two summers ago, but I can't. My mind won't let go of a static view in the window, as if it's holding me together.

Around noon, Jenna, my pretty neighbor friend, breaks into my silent grief. She's come to fetch me, as always on Fridays, to help organize and cook for the hot dog sale at our children's school.

"Are you okay?" she asks, and I nod yes.

We walk our usual route along the side streets until tears roll down my cheeks faster than I can stop them, and Jenna gently insists we turn back.

Once home again, she stays with me. My hands shake as I tearfully read her the letter, then show her the envelope with the postmark indicating that Bethie had mailed it the day before she died.

Jenna understands the value of a quiet, listening presence, having lost her sister Anne Marie last summer. She hands me tissues as I continue weeping while trying to talk to her, then give up, blow my nose, and sip the tea she has made for me.

Now more composed, I tell Jenna, "I should've known Bethie would end her own life, that she would carefully plan the whole thing, of course, in genius style. She *was* a genius. We all knew at least that much about her." My hand is shaking as I point again to the postmark on the envelope. "See this? Bethie sent me this before she died. Probably saw herself able to predict my reactions."

"I can tell you're angry," Jenna answers. "And probably her other friends got letters and are angry, too. Do you know some of them you could call?"

"She hardly had any friends. I think just Greta Shulberg and me. If you can call me a friend. We used to be very close. In high school and college, Bethie meant so much to me. But I haven't really been her friend these last few years." Sobbing again, I painfully confess, "At Bethie's last visit, she said things... things I didn't want to hear. I prompted her to leave and she did. I didn't phone her or write after that. I don't know what happened to her. Why would she...? Her aunt said she took a lot of pills. But why?"

"Maybe her other friend knows."

"I suppose I could call Greta. Bethie phoned her from our house. I remember writing down Greta's number in my address book because Bethie said if I'm ever in New York, I should look her up."

When Mark comes home from work, I manage to pull myself together and show him Bethie's letter.

"What's this all about? I don't get it," he says.

"It means she's gone, Mark. She's dead."

"Suicide? Good God, I can't believe..." He sees I'm starting to lose control and adds, "Well, she was always kinda nuts, Carol." Mark reaches out, probably to offer comfort, but his judging of Bethie angers me. I back away and go upstairs.

For a while I sit in our bedroom rocker, finding solace in the dark silence. I whisper Bethie's name again and again, wishing she would somehow answer. If spirits had a way of speaking, I think Bethie's would be trying to tell me something. Why else would she send me a letter just before she died?

I can hear Wendy and Daniel go into the kitchen downstairs. Mark is saying something to them. Then Wendy cries out, "No, not Mom's friend Bethie!"

Soon Wendy is beside me, hugging and sobbing. How will I tell her how Bethie died? More than anything now, I want to comfort her, and I try, but my own grief spills into her and we're both crying. We lie down on the bed together in each other's arms and she soon falls asleep. Seeing her beautiful young face looking peaceful again comforts me. I finger away the traces of her tears and wonder again how I'll be able to tell her how Bethie died. Soon she'll probably ask. Maybe Mark has already told her.

When Mark comes upstairs, I'm still holding her. He says, "I'll take Wendy and put her to bed now, Carol." He takes her from me and lifts her up into his arms. "She has school tomorrow and you need to rest. Try to sleep, okay?" He carries her to her bed.

When he returns and climbs into bed, he gathers my limp body close to him.

The day after the arrival of Bethie's shocking letter, I begin writing cinquains, the five-line stanzas with syllables in the patterned, classic form that Professor Hallikis taught us in the poetry seminar we attended together ten years ago when we were students at the University of Chicago.

I continue late into the night writing my cinquains to Bethie, as if these small clusters of five-line poems might somehow replace the flowers I never put on her grave or the words I never spoke to her as a friend. Their vertical and horizontal pattern on the page remind me of flowers, long-stemmed roses of various lengths, laid across a table or on a grave.

Did you
At the crossroad
Standing in the darkness
Stretch one arm through your agony
For me?

Will my cinquains to Bethie someday provide data in a bio of me? I can imagine an apt description of the famous poet Carol Mandell Simon's cinquains to her friend: A NECESSARY OBSESSION TO ASSUAGE GUILT.

Is there a law of motion that explains why I'm writing these cinquains to her and am planning to light a memorial candle? Is there a difference between tradition and an obsession? When people we love come into our lives, suppose they never totally leave. Perhaps, as an extension of Newton's laws, their every action has an equal and opposite reaction in our hearts, and now it's as if Bethie chose me to keep her spirit alive by remembering what we shared and trying to understand what led to her tragic decision.

Was it
one angry wish
or some unsettled debt
to stamp forever on our heads
regret?

TWO

On the day of Bethie's funeral, I decide to walk along the beach at Newport Bay hoping to catch a view of the sun at the place where it disappears suddenly into the sea, a sight that has always fascinated me. Today, though, it reminds me of my own life, how it seems to move in a patterned motion also, and I again consider that all of us may be more intimately involved than we realize in the same basic laws of motion as the moon and stars. Maybe there are actual formulas that could even describe our plans, and what seems secret or impossible to know might someday be explained in the college physics class by a smarter generation.

I arrive home inspired by such speculation and, even though tired enough for a nap, I hurry to prepare supper with leftovers.

Later, folding my three children with their usual shenanigans into their beds, I light the 24-hour memory candle I'd stopped to purchase on my way home, and for a while, I try to ignore its dim, lonely look on the fireplace mantel, but soon I find myself hovering over it and wondering if it will last its advertised promise.

After Mark leaves for his weekly poker game with his friends, I curl up on the sofa beside the mantel and become absorbed in memories of Bethie. Maybe I bought this traditional Jewish memorial candle to watch its flame flicker before my eyes and call back her life into mine. As I stare into its soft light, I notice how much the flame resembles the color of her hair, long and thick, its golden brilliance falling down her back and swishing from side to side as we walked together along the corridors of La Mesa High. I close my eyes and we are together there again.

Everyone calls Bethie "weirdo brain." I'm her only friend.

At first, I, too, am suspicious of her peculiarly piercing green eyes and the radical ideas she flaunts with outrageous confidence. The role assigned to us as teenage girls is to act always as if somewhat in need. What that need is doesn't matter as long as we keep it in modest, attractive boundaries.

Bethie, however, will not play her part. She asks to be given exams so she can avoid "unnecessary courses." When her request is refused, at the end of her freshman year, she brings the results of private testing she has undertaken that show her readiness for college. Although the tests actually prove her readiness, she learns that no university will accept her for at least two years.

One day during English class, Bethie tells several members of our football team sitting at the back of the room making ugly noises that she thinks they exhibit behavior more characteristic of the canine species. "Specifically," she suggests, "someone throws a ball and you run for it, and then there's your sniffing after females for sexual release." After she spoke, they looked at her in shock.

Bethie has designed several multiple-choice surveys and passes them around to a sampling of students. "To test certain of my hypotheses on a variety of topics," she eagerly explained to Mr.

White, our superintendent. When told to desist from her independently motivated scientific endeavors, she tells him that she plans to continue this activity off campus until she's gathered all the data she needs.

This year Bethie and I are invited to join a special creative writing class. We both write poetry, and I've come to think of myself as a poet, a good or bad one depending on outside critiques, but Bethie always claims she uses a formula and isn't really serious about her poems or what anyone thinks about them.

One day, I see that one of her poems, "Masks & After" was published by a small college press, so I stop by the lunch table where she always sits alone to tell her I saw her poem and say how much I like it. She looks so beautiful, even just dressed in blue jeans and sweater, her long, strawberry-blonde hair falling to her waist.

I sit down next to her with my lunch tray, and soon we're discussing her poem. She then proudly announces it's one of her many "formula poems" written only to gain credits toward winning a scholarship and early admittance to The University of Chicago.

"What's the formula?" I ask.

When she hesitates to answer, I offer to share the slice of my mother's prizewinning marble cake I'd brought even though my sister Molly warned me not to eat it. She accuses our Mom of baking rich cakes to make us fat like her.

"Okay! It's a deal. That cake looks deliciously evil," Bethie says as she reaches for the slightly bigger piece.

"So what's the formula for your poem?"

"It's easy," she boasts, licking frosting off her fingers. Then, businesslike, she begins her how-to steps, which remind me of the instructions on how to put together the doll house I built for my little cousin Minny: First, you find a flat surface, etc.

Bethie begins with, "First I sit at my desk, close my eyes and focus on some word."

"What was your focus word for the published one? Was it *masks* or *after?*"

"I don't remember."

"Come on. Please," I beg, wanting her to explain a scheme that could produce a poem like that one. "I need help with some of mine. Tell me."

"All right. I focused on the word *masks*. Then on to step two, I visualize the idea word in a concrete form. You know, like a black mask with two holes."

"What did you see then?" I lean forward, fascinated.

"A smile, of course. That's what brought me to think *laughter.*"

"How about the next four lines?"

"What are they," she challenges, "if you think they're so great?"

I recite them from memory:

> Our house was beautiful and gay;
> No friend or guest would ever know
> How when they left our homey show,
> All our laughter fell away.

"Notice the rhyme pattern," she instructs.

"Line l with line 4; line 2 with line 3. Unusual? No. To capture the simple irony of the relationship as between the two rhymed words. The next four lines are an extended example of that irony."

"So doesn't the poet need to tell what's masked?"

"No." With her eyes cast down, Bethie suddenly turns away while responding, "The poet doesn't want to tell that. She loves wearing the mask. It gives her privacy. The more she wears it, the more it becomes her, and soon she's really laughing underneath the mask."

I bend closer and she turns back to me smiling, and says, "The conclusion should reflect a return to the beginning theme. It's as easy as that." Smiling more broadly now, she eats the last bits of Mom's cake, then grabs her books and hurries off to her next class.

I round the corner of the hallway leading to my next class thinking to myself, *Who's she trying to kid? That's no formula poem. She meant every word of it.*

My first clue that Bethie and her family have secrets.

If I hadn't seen Bethie's poem in my cousin's college magazine, we might never have become friends. Or are two poets in the same room bound to attract? Are there laws of human emotion, like the law of inertia? Maybe we continue doing whatever we do until a stronger force acts upon us and prevails. Certainly, I feel strongly attracted to Bethie's genius and whatever causes it to prevail over the opinions of my friends and classmates. Her strong ideas both shock and fascinate me. She's brilliant and willing to talk to me about anything.

Well, almost.

We decide to leave the cafeteria area and begin searching for a quieter place to spend our lunch hour. "Why don't we ever talk about our mothers?" I ask, wanting to share painful thoughts about mine with her.

When we walk by the table where my sister Molly and her friends sit, we hear snickering and laughter, which makes us even more determined to seek refuge. We notice an area behind the patio trees and hurry to find a spot suitable for sitting and unloading our books.

"Let's talk about our fathers," Bethie offers while we munch on our sandwiches. "Mine's a lawyer. His name is Meyer Hartung. He was a well-known lawyer in Austria, but he left before the war. Now he has an office attached to our home and just a few clients. What does your dad do?"

"He's a carpenter. Came here from Russia in 1938 with his mother, brother and his sister, Caroline, who got sick soon after that and died. I'm named after her. My dad is also a Talmudic scholar. He reads Hebrew fluently from the scrolls every Saturday at our synagogue."

"Ask him to teach me. I want to know everything and try everything."

"Everything? Wouldn't some of that be dangerous?" Scenes invade my mind of Bethie climbing Ayers Rock, Bethie in drug orgies, blood rituals. I try to erase them, but her green eyes are sparkling with excitement, keeping me fascinated and imagining more scenes.

"Yes," she laughs. "Dangerous is wonderful!"

We're too different, I tell myself. How do we stay friends?

I try to believe this will happen, that maybe as opposites, we're drawn to one another, our positive and negative polarities acting as electrical charges on our energy systems in accord with certain laws that channel hormonal-like clusters into our feelings.

Maybe this theory, if someday statistically validated, will explain, predict, even assist in the avoidance of loss.

I write another cinquain to Bethie; its syllabic pattern seems like a floral arrangement I'm bringing her and its prescribed form seems a comfort.

You were
of torch and flame
I only candle light
and yet I walked beside you as
a friend.

THREE

I'm proud of my friendship with Bethie, and I tell that to my sister, Molly. She laughs at me and then proceeds to issue her big-sister commands.

"Don't hang with her, Carol. No one likes her. She's weird," Molly warns in her most self-assured tone, as if the quality of her information should not be questioned since she was potty trained before I was born.

Lack of agreement by a younger sibling is hardly ever tolerated in our crowd. With brothers, like Eddie and Frank Hanover, very significant punching would be involved following any unheeded direction from the older sibling to the younger. Last year I saw what happened in the school yard when Eddie talked back to Frank in front of everyone. One good punch or two, a bloody nose, a black eye, and it was over. A strong show of forceful pride by an older boy usually keeps a younger one in line from then on.

So it seems with boys.

Not so with girls.

For us, it's verbal from start to finish. If a younger or even a less popular girl answers back, it begins a word war that continues as the stronger willed girl, often a leader like Molly, carries on the tirade of abusive insults day after day. Finally, the younger or weaker girl wears down, cries, and runs from continually abusive confrontations until, in desperation, she seeks teacher or parental intervention, which might put a stop to it, but more likely won't. I learned early that the best way for me to win verbal warfare is to befriend silence.

"Don't hang out with her!" Molly commands again. "All my friends say she's sex crazy. Barbara saw her with some sailor guy one day. She's only fifteen, but Barbara says her clothes made her look like a whore."

Your friends are all dumb! I whisper this to myself as I slowly back away and turn my eyes in the direction of an escape path while waving at no one in particular in a crowd nearby, and then I'm off without looking back.

Molly, it seems, *is* really smarter than all her friends, which is a good thing in a way. It gives her leadership qualities. She tells me that all her friends except her read only the abridged versions of the classics and they work happily in the "Notions" section of Woolworth's so they can get discounts on lipsticks. "I'm so bored selling mothballs and hangers every Saturday," she admits, "but Barbara and Saundra don't mind. I'm just putting up with it for the discounts."

Even though Molly doesn't do well in school, she knows our high school social scene much better than I do. Her good looks, inherited from our Polish maternal grandmother, and her self-confidence win her popularity with girls and boys. She's now president of her class.

Molly is our mother's favorite.

"Nobody's going to pull the wool over my Molly's eyes," Mom often says. "She's our golden Jewish girl star."

Mom loves Molly's blonde hair. She can't help expressing her adoration of it with family and friends, and each time, my very dark brown, almost black hair seems to lose some of its luster, though I can't tell why. I don't really want blonde hair. It usually looks streaked with other colors, except for a few of the little girls in our Temple nursery school. Now even Molly has taken to bleaching her hair when the darker roots begin to appear. But Mom keeps on worshiping it and glancing over at mine, probably making an effort to say nothing. Maybe I'm just imagining all this. Although once, still bearing the brave truthfulness of innocence, I reminded her, "Mine is like yours, Mommy," and got a hard stare. From then on, I made silence an even closer ally.

Our father rarely speaks with Molly. They don't seem to have much to say to each other. When they try, it seems funny to me the way it often turns out.

Like last year during Purim, a festive Jewish holiday, Dad asked, "Molly, come with Carol and me to hear *The Book of Esther*. We'll read from it tonight at temple. It's a beautiful story."

"Sorry, can't, Dad. Have to give Barbara a perm."

"*The Book of Esther* is thousands of years old, Mol."

"Sorry. It'll have to wait a little longer then."

Dad doesn't have a favorite. We both understand why. It's wrong because it makes trouble between siblings.

He often talks of Cain and Abel, Jacob and Esau, and Joseph, whose father, Jacob, gave him the special coat-of-many-colors that caused his brothers to hate him.

"Jacob had no business doing that," Dad says. "He set in motion the hatred of his brothers against him."

Dad speaks of Joseph's many-colored coat as if he's still angered by it now, thousands of years later. "Our forefathers weren't perfect, little Carol. They made a lot of trouble among their own and for generations after. Look what has happened with Isaac and Ishmael? Jews and Arabs became enemies instead of brother nations."

I love hearing Dad talk about God and the Bible.

If my father allowed himself a favorite, it would probably be me. That might help me to sometimes forget how much Mom hates me. I can tell. She scares me, and I want to hate her too, but that's even more scary.

Regardless of Molly's later warnings that her friends whisper ugly things about us, I continue to meet Bethie at lunch time. We eat in the patio area, sitting on the steps leading into the auditorium, where, from our marginal perspective, we feel free to observe and discuss the various hero and heroine peers dominating our high school scene. We sit there usually unnoticed, comparing impressions, reading our poems to each other, and talking about our classes and teachers.

Most people, including teachers, seem incredibly dumb to Bethie. I don't always agree, but she loves it when I do.

"How about Miss D.?" I ask. It was Bethie's idea that we call her that because her name, Miss Dittlebaum, is a source of ridicule among our fellow students. I thought it was a great idea, so we asked her if it was okay, and since she didn't object, Miss D. soon became her name to everyone in our creative writing class.

She always inspires us with intriguing assignments. Even Bethie.

"She's definitely not dumb," Bethie admits.

"Why doesn't she like you?" We've both concluded this because Miss D. hardly ever calls on Bethie.

"She's not comfortable with assertive...well, okay with outspoken girls like me. I probably make her feel ashamed because she isn't able to speak up for herself. Remember how she backed off when they cut the yearbook budget? She didn't protest even though I heard her tell Tim Pendleton, our student editor, that she was angry about it but didn't want to make waves with the super."

"I guess she has to think about her job, too."

"Anyway, she loves you, Carol. I'll bet she was a lot like you when she was a girl."

"Really?"

I feel proud hearing Bethie say that. Miss D. is my favorite teacher. I want to be like her. "But she knows how smart you are and she respects you," I assure Bethie. She likes hearing that. I don't tell her that both Miss D. and I don't appreciate her bragging about her so-called "formula" poems.

Girls like Bethie and me, who like to discuss literature and philosophy and history, are not popular at our school, so most of us keep our opinions to ourselves, but Bethie doesn't hide hers. She delights in showing her genius in any way. Still, she longs to be accepted and probably feels hurt when rejected by our classmates.

We often spend part of our lunch hour sharing each other's pain, and sometimes we even succeed in laughing it away for a while.

"When I first came to La Mesa High as a freshman," Bethie confides, "I had new hopes of not always being an outcast."

"Were you feeling left out when you were little?"

She nods. "Let me tell you about my worst day in kindergarten. My father helped me make a small model of The Globe Theater for Show and Tell, and I began to recite lines from *Macbeth* to go along with my project. 'Out, out damned spot.' It shocked the teacher so much she shouted, 'That's enough, Elizabeth! Sit down.' I wanted to cry then, but I didn't."

I imagine Bethie's little face ablaze with shame when she sat down to the giggles of her classmates.

"After school, they gathered around me, and some started chanting 'Out, out damn spot'... probably the first and last time they spoke a word of Shakespeare," she says bitterly.

"So you were called Elizabeth at school then. When did you become Bethie?"

"Not until junior high. My parents called me Bethie some-times, so I thought it would sound cute, you know, more friend-ly, like the other kids' names. Ruth Dunning was called Ruthie and Barbara Schultz was called Bunny. In 7th grade, I asked all my teachers to call me Bethie."

"Did that help?"

"At first. Until the principal, Mr. Wyman, came into science class and the fool announced to the teacher and all of us that I was skipping seventh grade and going on to eighth grade immediately, and he beckoned me to follow him out of the class."

"What happened then?"

"Guess. The seventh-graders were jealous and the eighth- graders were insulted. Recess became everyone-harass-Bethie time."

"I couldn't have survived. But you did. How?"

"By knowing the enemy. Being prepared. I was already an avid reader of adolescent psychology books. My father gave me a pile of them when I was ten. He said I'd need them. As always, he was right."

"How did they help?"

"When I studied about them, I understood the whole, silly peer group ignorance, which is why the name didn't help. I'm too different to be helped by a name change. But you have a great name. Carol sounds friendly but also like the makings of a strong woman." She's smiling and now, so am I. We both know I have trouble being strong. Compared to her, I qualify as one of the meek, Biblically speaking, who can only hope to be assigned to some kind of later inheritance. I often wonder why Bethie likes me. Maybe it's because I'm the only one who seems to give her brilliant ideas an appreciative audience.

"I was named after my aunt Caroline, my dad's sister," I tell Bethie. "She died before I was born. My dad really loved her a lot, but Molly remembers that Aunt Caroline was kind of mean sometimes to our mom because she didn't like her. So, I'm guessing Mom must have hated Aunt Caroline."

"Then why name you...?"

"My dad insisted that at least I be given her Hebrew name, Chaya, which means "life" in Hebrew. And lucky for me, Mom wouldn't go for that in English. Molly says Mom told her that her girls had to have English names like other American girls. Anyway, she agreed to name me Carol. My dad loves both my names. I guess they remind him of Caroline. Mom still doesn't seem to like my name even though 'Carol' seems American enough."

After we finish our lunch, as we walk toward the music building, I feel crampy and sick to my stomach. "I'd better see the nurse," I say, pressing my stomach. "I don't feel good. You'd better go on to class without me."

"I'll tell Mr. Reinhart you're at sick-of-the-month-club."

"Don't!"

"Kidding. Only kidding."

In the school nurse's office, I tell her I'm having cramps and feel sick to my stomach. She has me lie down on a cot.

"I'll be right back with a hall pass and you can go home."

I wait for her to return from the principal's office next door to the infirmary. Our school, with its modern, Southwest design, was built quickly to accommodate the sudden growth in population resulting from new, more affordable homes built following the war. Consequently, the walls are so thin we can hear what goes on in the adjacent classrooms and offices. When Brenda Martin, our nurse, speaks with Mrs. Gorman, our vice-principal, I overhear their entire conversation as I lie on the narrow cot along the wall shared with the office next door.

"Hi, Brenda. How's it going?"

"Slow today. Yesterday I was really busy. I've got Carol Mandell in the infirmary now. She's got The Curse. Wants to go home. She doesn't look good. She should go."

"Okay." A pause. To write the pass, I'm guessing. Then footsteps sound along the wall and stop suddenly, and I hear Vice-Principal Gorman's voice again.

"Carol Mandell. Isn't she the girl who's buddy-buddy with Bethie Hartung? Miss Know-it-all Hartung. She's the one with the scientific theories and written tests she once asked permission to distribute."

"Yes. So arrogant. Too smart for her own good, I guess. It always gets her in trouble with staff. The kids don't like her either."

"What about Carol? Do you think they're a couple?"

"Hard to tell. But they do seem close. They sit out there in the patio alone every day during lunch hour. Always just the two of them."

When Nurse Brenda opens her office door a moment later, she finds me standing in front of her.

"We aren't a couple," I say, glaring at her, and while seeing her eyes opened wide with surprise, I suddenly vomit over both of us. She hurries me to the sink and holds my head while I vomit again.

"It usually happens twice," she says as she wipes my face with a cool, wet towel.

After we clean ourselves up as best we can, she sits me down again on the cot and asks, "Are you okay now, do you think?" I nod, feeling less sick but embarrassed.

"We're not a couple," I manage to repeat.

"No," she agrees while eagerly handing me the pass.

Once home, I sit in the big rocking chair in the bedroom I share with Molly, feeling grateful for a few hours of time alone before she comes bouncing in with one of her friends. Soon the scene

I overheard in the nurse's office comes flooding back. I tell myself they had no right to their wild suspicions about Bethie and me.

Still upset, I grab my worn, brown teddy bear to hug for comfort. We rock while my mind travels back there and I review what happened at Camp Bluebrook the summer when I was ten.

When Cathy and Muriel overstay free time while picking blueberries together and come back an hour late for our craft projects, they're immediately sent to the cabin of the camp director, Uncle Mike, for a talk with Aunt Hildy, his wife. She's the kind lady who takes care of their baby boy, and she helps us with various activities.

Cathy and Muriel emerge from Uncle Mike's cabin with their eyes red from crying. They don't look at each other during dinner, and for a few nights afterward I hear Muriel, who sleeps on the cot next to me, crying softly into her pillow. I want to go to her, but I don't know what to say. Then, on visiting day, Muriel goes home with her parents without saying goodbye to any of us, not even Cathy, her best friend.

A week later, on the bus going home, I sit next to Cathy, and she tells me about the berry-picking they did so the camp cook would make us all a pie for dinner, and how that made them late for crafts, and Uncle Bob took away their free time together for the rest of the session, which made Muriel want to leave camp on visiting day.

"We weren't doing anything bad," she says.

"I believe you." And to prove it, I give her the Indian bracelet I made during crafts that day. She hugs me and puts it on.

An innocent friendship, distorted by some kind of adult

judgment I can't understand, certainly not then as a ten-year-old girl, and not even now as I lie on my bed the rest of the afternoon, trying to separate myself from the sting.

Soon I'm hearing Molly's voice and then footsteps coming up the stairs.

"Hi, Baby Sister," Molly says from the doorway with Barbara Koffer, her best friend. "Why are you home in bed?"

"Sick," I reply. "I vomited on me and the school nurse. She sent me home." They both laugh hysterically. It's easy to amuse them with a story about messing over an adult.

Barbara, still giggling, suggests, "Let's get out of here. Get your records. We can play them at my house."

When they leave, I recall a time when Mom didn't like Barbara and forbade Molly to spend the night with her ever again.

"But, Mom," Molly tried to explain, "we baby-sit her little brother Kenny. Her parents count on us. And they leave us Cokes and potato chips..."

Mom grew angrier. "No! Not without parents there. I saw you two go into the bathroom together and lock the door. No! No more monkey business."

Molly had stormed off to our bedroom, and I wanted to ask Mom about "monkey business," but I knew better. She left the kitchen too upset to talk.

Later, I asked Molly, "What's monkey business?"

"None of your damn business, so just shut up!"

Soon after that, Molly and Barbara started talking constantly about boys, curling each other's hair, wearing lipstick and polishing each other's nails.

"We have to get ready for high school," Molly firmly announced. "And soon, we'll be going out with boys."

Mom didn't mind that, and she now even likes Barbara.

The next day during lunch, when I tell Bethie about my ordeal in the nurse's office, my education about "monkey business" begins. She gives me the unabridged story about coupling among girls.

"Don't look so shocked, Carol. Girls know how to make love to each other, too."

"But can you imagine how anyone would think of us as a couple?"

"Yes," she replies, lifting her squashed cupcake from its cellophane bag and licking melted chocolate from her fingers. "Truly, I can."

I watched in silence as she finishes her cake and washes it down with a Coke. Then, unable to contain my surprise any longer, I confront her. "How can you imagine anything like that between us?" She leans toward me smiling, her green eyes so wide, I feel myself sailing into them. I lean away.

"You're so pretty, Carol. I sometimes imagine us…"

My cheeks flush with embarrassment.

"Tell me you're joking!"

Still smiling, she just shrugs.

I stand up and grab for my books, relieved to hear the lunch bell insist it's time to go to our next class.

FOUR

For weeks after Bethie's letter came, I try to cope with my grief within the daily requirements of family life. I want to settle back into my previous activities, but everything has changed, taking on a new heaviness. What I once called projects are now tasks. Sex is even more like passionless ritual to keep Mark happy, and I'm convinced he doesn't truly love me. Like a prostitute, I'm giving him what he wants so he won't lose interest, find someone else and want a divorce.

Overwhelmed by even the basics of caring for our home and three children, I've dropped my few commitments that extend to the outside world. My children are feeling the new distance my grief has laid between us. I'm noticing their downcast eyes while I speak to them only to give orders or make requests, and my heart aches to see them hurting when my distracted state of mind appears to them as indifference. Sometimes I think they start fighting as their way of begging me to interfere, but I can't seem to get control of the situation. Once Daniel pinched little Judd and then looked over at me with a devilish grin. Wendy immediately came to rescue Judd when she heard him cry out. She slapped Daniel until he cried and ran from the room. "He can't do that to our baby," Wendy said, her worried face searching mine for guidance, but I only managed a nod and smile when hearing her call little Judd "our baby."

Now, each morning, after Mark gets Wendy and Daniel off to school and takes Judd to nursery school, I sit at the kitchen table, still in my robe, and daydream away most of the morning until it's time to pick up Judd. Instead of doing chores and planning dinner, I think of the trips I might have taken with Bethie if only Mark and I had decided to take separate vacations. I imagine us traveling up the coast together and staying in little beach towns, chatting with the locals, painting or taking photos as we go, then each writing and sharing our poems. That's really all I want to do now, instead of trying to make everything around here work for Mark and the kids. What has happened to me? Bethie was right. I'm just a poet who hardly writes anymore, a dancer who doesn't dance, a journalist who doesn't even have time to read the paper, and now I'm not even being a good mother.

I make myself some tea and then get dressed to take a walk, hoping it will make me feel better. But then I can't even push myself out the door. I sit back down with another cup of tea, thinking I should try to eat something even if I'm not hungry, but that would take more energy. All I seem to be able to do is sit here and remember Bethie and when we were together.

* * *

At the University of Chicago, we sit in front of Cobb Hall discussing our Humanities II class when Professor Halikis read from the story "How Beautiful With Shoes," his voice seeming to come from another more wonderful world than ours.

"The Greek Isles," Bethie suggests. "That's the place. Let's plan to go there. When do you think we can leave?"

"Soon," I lie, knowing she feels lonely and caged in by the conventions of campus life. I want to comfort her as she has often comforted me while I'm worrying about so many things. "Maybe we can go right after graduation."

I haven't yet told Bethie that Mark and I are planning to elope at Spring Break. We've decided to keep it a secret. But even if that never happened, I'm afraid to travel with Bethie. Her brave mind always extends far beyond mine. I used to wish I could be that way, but lately I'm glad I'm not.

She's fascinated with James Dean movies and rock bands like the Grateful Dead, making the scene after President Kennedy's assassination. And soon after, Janis Joplin and Jimi Hendrix images parade all over the dorms. Bethie listens to The Who. In their famous album *My Generation,* she loves to hear them sing that they hope to die before they get old. She's made that her mantra. Our generation is very aware of the constant threat of another war, possibly even a nuclear one, and the brave souls among us, like Bethie, seem to be fighting fear by taking their lives to the edge, testing and challenging everything their parents believe. I'm always amazed that Bethie and I stay friends since I've never been brave. How can a child afraid of her own mother be brave?

When I first realize Bethie's love of risk-taking is a regular part of her everyday life, we are still in high school. Her father has given her fifty dollars for her sixteenth birthday, and she wants us to use it to celebrate by going to Chez Cezanne, a little French restaurant near enough to her home that we can walk there and come back to her house on our own.

We arrive all dressed up and wearing make-up, and she tells the hostess, in French, that we'd made reservations. We hadn't. Bethie quickly glances down the list, picks out a woman's name and says, "Oh, there I am. That's me with reservations for two."

After we're seated and order our dinners, two women in expensive-looking suits and high heels walk in. They soon become loudly agitated. "But we made a reservation a week ago," the taller one insists. The hostess checks the list again and says she's sorry but there's no record of it. Apparently, the hostess crossed off Bethie's assumed name before she seated us. The women stalk off in anger while Bethie eyes me and, with a quiet giggle, butters her roll.

Too upset with her to enjoy my dinner, I whisper over our salads, "Suppose the hostess hadn't eradicated the evidence?"

"It always works. If you come early enough, the hostess forgets the name." Slightly ruffled by my discomfort, she urges, "Come on, Carol, you don't want to spoil my birthday, do you? No one died." I offer a half-smile to set things right between us.

"Carol, life is meant to be a series of adventures. I want to experience everything. Don't you?"

"Everything?" I test, not wanting to believe her.

"Yes," she says, her green eyes sparkling. "Boredom is *the* major cause of criminality, Carol."

The danger that Bethie attributed to boredom, could that cause a marriage to end? Maybe even cause someone to end their own life?

Now gone,
cannot say when
you first saw the dark glare
swallowing you into the mouth
of time

The worst times for me are now, late at night with everyone asleep. I'm alone, sitting at the kitchen table with a pot of tea and trying in vain to understand what happened to Bethie. She was so strong, yet she gave up, ended her life. If that happened to her, it could even more easily happen to me...the journey from the end of dreams to memories and then to nothingness.

First I tried to hold back such thoughts, afraid that if I let them loose, there'll be no way to stop them, but now, I'm aching for them to have their way with me, to gain strength, as if they're needed for the survival of our togetherness, and I want to feel nothing less than what Bethie suffered, to push myself weeping into the very last, loneliest hours I imagine were her life. No one in the next room to approach when hearing her call, to understand and share her pain, measured first in hours and days, then months of long nights with visions of time without end until a small, trembling light seeking closure shows her the way to the grave-- that invisible meeting place intersecting heart and silence, determined by the inappropriateness of dreams and how long until someone comes by.

And then, in one brief flicker of that dim light, I can feel myself standing with Bethie on the edge of her life, a place without seasons, only memories seeming to last for hours. Her features slowly take form, and I see her searching green eyes and her thick mounds of red hair streaked with gold. She looks exactly as I remember her-- as I always want to remember her. I call out to her, "Bethie, shall we rock together, friend, in and out of your darkness?"

When I finally lay my head on my arms at the kitchen table, I've been with Bethie's spirit, lighted by her memorial glass, and my mind dances from that reflection and back into the many days we spent together at La Mesa High.

FIVE

When I first meet Mr. Hartung, Bethie and I are working on a science project at her house. He comes into her room while we're sitting at her desk, and he sits down on her bed. I notice then how his eyes follow Bethie's every step as she moves around the room to find something, how he laughs at all her clever remarks, once even getting up, bending over her to kiss her cheek afterward, and how she smiles up at him.

Bethie's father doesn't seem to allow our biblical forefather's mistake to affect his obviously adoring attitude toward her. She wears the "coat of many colors" with the innocence of an only child.

Although he doesn't really know me, Mr. Hartung seems to like me immediately. I assume that's because I'm Bethie's friend. He probably thinks I'm as smart as she. I don't say much so he won't soon discover the truth. I just listen to their brilliant conversation, which inspires me to read all the sources they mention, to hold on to her friendship, which now means so much to me.

When the subject of religion comes up, they both declare immediately that they are atheists. I've never met even one openly announced atheist before, and they're a father-daughter team.

"Carol is being confirmed this year at her temple," Bethie tells him and adds with a big smile, "Well, we're confirmed atheists, aren't we, Dad?"

He agrees, turning to me with new interest and a look of sympathy. "Carol, at your age, confirming your faith is a lot to ask, isn't it?"

How does he know I feel pressured? "Well, boys commit at thirteen," I remind him. "At my confirmation ceremony, I'll be almost sixteen."

"Bar Mitzvah," he says, "Yes, I suppose a confirmation ceremony would have a similar effect. I've been told the Bar Mitzvah experience can be traumatic for some boys."

"Didn't you have one, Dad?"

"My parents decided it wasn't safe. The '30s were quite terrible years for German Jews. We saw shops being plundered, neighbors chased down the street naked. Our family didn't think about Bar Mitzvahs, just to blend in. But soon, no one with a Jewish background was safe. Not even their Christian friends were safe from the Nazis."

"My mother lost both her parents," Bethie says. "When the Nazis first occupied France, she and her brother and sister were sent to stay with an aunt in London, and soon after, her parents were sent to Auschwitz. My dad's parents barely escaped being arrested after being sold out to Nazi informers by some of their colleagues at Berlin University, to advance their careers."

"We don't know that with any certainty, Bethie," he reminds her, his knitted eyebrows signaling discomfort. She leans closer to touch his hand, then squeezes it.

"Lucky your parents left in time, right?"

"Right." He stands to leave and asks, "How about if I bring up the tray of oatmeal chocolate chip cookies I baked this morning?" When he sees my amazement, he assures me, "Yes, I did bake them, Carol. Leona goes to work early, but my office is here, so I have time for some culinary exploits." We all laugh at that.

When we taste and applaud his cookies, he announces jokingly, "Bethie will not bake cookies. She insists doing so would support a too confining female role."

Bethie's father doesn't need to worry like mine about causing trouble with favoritism. She'd told me that her mother's son from a previous marriage had died during games at a boarding school. Strange how Bethie calls him "my mother's son" instead of by his name.

While Bethie and I continue working together on our science project upstairs in her bedroom, our bodies sprawled alongside opened books and crunched paper, Mr. Hartung appears at the open door with a tray of Cokes, and asks, "How's the project coming, girls?"

I sit up quickly and look over my notes describing one of Newton's experiments and hope he'll ask to see only Bethie's notes. I'm not accustomed to parental involvement in homework. Bethie, however, seems very comfortable with it. She stays in her reclining position, delighted when he sets down the tray and pulls her, laughing, to a seated position.

"Look here, Dad," she points out. "This passage exemplifies Newton's pragmatic approach."

He sits down next to us and puts his arms around her while

reading over her shoulder. "Yes! Bethie, you've illuminated Newton's method in this context brilliantly."

I squirm beside them, feeling like an intruder, so intimate seems their delight in each other, and the way they are smiling has become strangely disturbing to me.

Thankful that Bethie's father hasn't asked about my notes, I put them away and stand up to go. He stands up also, and saying he has a client coming, he leaves.

"Don't go, Carol," Bethie urges. I sit back down and we continue to study and discuss Newton's Laws of Motion.

SIX

It's the spring of 1962, around the time when all Arizona schools soon let out early because the terrible heat threatens the possibility of further learning, and I invite Bethie to my religious school's Confirmation service. However, she refuses to come, saying, "My dad and I can't really understand what obviously intelligent people see in religious rituals and ceremonials."

Then while we're standing in the hall waiting to go into our biology class, Bethie tells me that her father and she discussed my upcoming Confirmation and he thinks it's unfair to ask a fifteen-year-old to confirm a complicated matter like a belief in God.

"Do you want to do it?" she asks.

I shrug. I don't know what I want to do now that Bethie's father has so exactly focused me upon my troubled soul. For several weeks I've agonized over the question of my readiness for Confirmation. I want to be with my class and have the part in the ceremony that's expected of me, but I'm not sure that I can do that honestly.

Flooding my mind are questions about the nature of a God who would allow Hitler such evil power. Once I happened to see a little boy in the park who was so deformed he couldn't even hold up his own head, and from then on, I began hating with all my heart whatever may have caused his suffering. Surely not the God my father loved so much, I tried to reassure myself, but I couldn't stop thinking that if that was God's will, I could no longer pray to such a monster.

After a week of missing classes while suffering from severe headaches, I suddenly find relief in believing with Bethie and her father that God does not actually exist, in which case, all my thoughts would be private, and even my anger and hate would be safe from future punishments.

That hiatus, however, does not last.

When our class begins serious preparations for the big day when we'd be the first Confirmation class of the newest synagogue in Arizona, I'm still questioning if I should participate, thereby confirming my faith in front of the whole congregation in our beautiful sanctuary with its twelve woven tapestries representing the twelve tribes, which I think are almost as lovely as the twelve stained-glass Chagall windows that our class saw on film last year.

When I've built up enough courage to discuss the question with my father, we've just finished dinner and have settled down in the living room to turn on the news. Dad follows world events carefully, but I capture his immediate attention when I ask, "Dad, is it possible to be Jewish and not believe in God?"

"That's quite a question," he says, not seeming in the least startled by it, just nodding his head slowly and taking a moment to ponder.

"About God, Carol, we can't know anything certain. But we

must have faith, follow the laws, keep the commandments."

"But what if some people aren't certain there *is* a God? What if they have serious doubts? Do you still think they should continue to say prayers?"

"It's very complicated, your question. Why do you ask all of this now? Is something wrong?"

When I explain why I'm not certain about going through with the Confirmation ceremony, he assures me it is not meant to be an end of my struggle to understand God, just a beginning.

"You see," he explains, "how your upcoming Confirmation is causing you to think much more about God."

Then, sounding more serious, he leans closer, saying, "Dear One, never separate yourself from our people. They are your mind's ancient connection with hope, your survival spirit."

Maybe it was what my father said or some cerebral exercise in psychic preservation that may someday be charted by regular and irregular brain waves (a process similar to what is done now with pulse rates to detect a lie), but I decide that if it's possible to have one's faith confirmed in a holy place, I should go through with the Confirmation ceremony and hope for, maybe even be prepared for, God's spirit to touch and transform me that day right there on the pulpit. It seems worth a try.

Each of us has been asked to give a short speech that reflects both study and faith. To my amazement, mine turns out to be a confessional as well as a memorial to the young Hungarian Jewish poet and freedom fighter Hannah Sennesh, who the Germans captured during a rescue mission and executed after she refused to give them any information.

I'd learned about Hannah's heroism by chance while leafing through Bethie's book about Jewish women poets. We'd taken turns reading all of Hannah's poems to each other that afternoon, and I discovered then that one of her poems is now a famous Jewish prayer sung each year during the High Holy Days.

"I wonder why my Confirmation class never studied about Hannah. She was so brave and wrote such beautiful poetry," I remarked as we laid the book aside.

"Because Jewish girls aren't admired for their bravery or their verse," Bethie answered, echoing my own newly awakened bitterness and doubt.

I decided then to write my confirmation speech to reflect my admiration for Hannah. "At least, I'll be saying something I truly feel," I told Bethie.

"What a great idea!" she said. "Go for it, Carol."

On the evening of the Confirmation service, our whole class stands together dressed in white graduation robes for the traditional picture that will later hang for generations in the temple foyer. If ever I forget the anxiety about the occasion building in me over these last few weeks of testing, rehearsals, and speechwriting, this picture will become a stark reminder. My face will look drawn and stiff, my smile too tight.

Ironically, I've been chosen to give the valedictory address since I earned the highest grade on the final exam. My speech is really a poem, but since it doesn't rhyme, it received our rabbi's approval.

At the lectern, I adjust the microphone and begin:

"For generations, someone's child
has cried out in the dark
asking the same lonely questions:
Who am I? Where am I going?
And for generations, someone's child
turned her face to the wall,
would not see and be named.

"And I, too, turned my face to the wall,
would not see and be named.
I went as one who was fluid,
letting my life flow freely
over the long, silent grooves of
generation... I wanted to cut
the numbers off my survival.
I would not be baked or tied,
all given away to causes.
I would not be laid in a box
all frozen like Hannah Sennesh
who died fighting for freedom.
Hannah wrote, 'At the crossroad,
I covered my ears with frost
and wept for what I had lost.'

"Hannah, brave Hannah,
I cry in your darkness now too;
send our rivers of anger
over frozen hills and curse
the beast who stung your eyelids shut,
and I'm asking your same lonely questions;
Who am I? Where am I going?
Am I named now? Chosen
to sleep at the crossroads with you?"

For a few minutes, seeming forever, I stand frozen in the silence following my speech. Then I sit back down next to my classmates.

As they, one by one, rise to give their speeches, I notice how different they sound from their usual lively, slang chatter before classes. Now, they each speak thoughtfully. Some quote our biblical forefathers; others recite the wisdoms of famous scholars; all make promises in keeping with the commandments. At the end of each of their speeches, applause fills the sanctuary. *But why not for me? Did I say something wrong?*

I feel so painfully alone now, even in the midst of my teachers, friends and family.

When we line up to receive congratulations, my father kisses me, and a few others give me a smile or squeeze my hand. I don't remember my mother being in that line, but she must have attended the Confirmation service because later when we're having refreshments, I *do* remember her there asking me how I could admit to "such foolish ideas," and then adding that she hopes my Confirmation will help me to "finally grow up."

Before we leave, Mom hands me a carefully wrapped box, my Confirmation gift. It's a watch without numbers, just time markings, and a pretty gold stretch band, the one I'd mentioned to Molly that I saw and liked.

I thank Mom, give Dad a quick hug, and put the watch on. Then I look for Molly in the crowd to show it to her, and I discover she's already left with her friends.

At home, when I show Molly the watch, she says, "Mine's a lot nicer, but that's what you wanted."

"I love it," I say. "Thanks for letting Mom and Dad know."

I run upstairs to our room and throw myself across my bed, and soon a sadness I don't understand envelops and caresses me while I cry quietly into my pillow.

Later, I play back our Confirmation ceremony in my mind, and can understand its strange dynamic: probably my classmates were like a beloved chorus that our community of parents and teachers must have been waiting to hear after I'd concluded my very non-traditional poem solo.

At school the following Monday, I tell Bethie about it all. She shakes her head. "Well, what did you expect?"

"Not this." I show her my new watch. "It was so expensive. I didn't count on them buying it for me."

"Hey, you deserve it," she insists, confirming at least my faith in our friendship.

SEVEN

Could anyone have predicted Bethie's suicide? I still wonder about that.

Suppose that in a matter of minutes, a whole series of data on her life were produced and entered into images on some kind of disk labeled *Elizabeth Hartung*. Even that train ride she described, when she and her parents were coming home from her brother's funeral, and sitting on her father's lap, she heard her mother weeping while he told his little girl, with new affection, "Now you are all we have." Next, a graph might appear on the same disk showing how her heartbeat changed at that moment from one quieted with sorrow to a quickness of pulse out of the normal range for a young child.

We are on the steps of the music building during lunch hour when Bethie describes a strange blending of fear and pleasure beginning that day on the train when she was seven years old.

"That feeling," she confides as we walk together to our geometry class, "well, it's a kind of pleasure to me now. I like it." Smiling, her eyes seem animated with those thoughts.

"I don't know what you mean," I tell her.

"Sure you do," she laughs. "It feels sexy."

Seeing my confused expression, she continues, "Check out this name in any good dictionary: Marquis de Sade. His dates are 1740 to 1814." She moves quickly ahead of me, tossing a thick length of her reddish golden hair over her shoulder as she hurries into the classroom.

Always jealous of her vast general knowledge, I hurry over to the huge dictionary on a table in the corner of the classroom and quickly look up Sade. I'm referred to the word "sadism" and then to elaborations dealing with sexual cruelty and forms of punishment.

When I finish reading the definitions, I glance up and see Bethie watching me from her desk. Her cheeks look flushed, and I read her lips saying to me, "I like…"

I turn away quickly, not wanting to know more.

During class, I can't let go of the dictionary definitions. They bring back my ugly feelings at a family punishment scene I want to forget but sometimes, like now, is triggered to replay.

Molly coming home late for supper. Mom saying Molly won't be going anywhere for a while. Molly crying that Mom never lets her be like her friends. Mom backing her chair away from the table while still sitting in it, then spreading her fat knees, her flowered dress riding up above them.

"Come here!" she angrily says to Molly, "I'll give you something to cry about!" She grabs Molly before she can run and pulls her over her knees. Molly's bottom is laid bare. Mom smacks and smacks while I stand wide-eyed. Molly cries until Mom stops, and I see Molly's bottom is red with punishment.

Mom looks at me. "Now you know what happens to bad girls." I nod a definite yes, and with spasms of agonizing fear exploding inside me as never before, I run out into the yard gasping for air.

Afterward, Molly goes to Dad and he comforts her with a kiss. I'm jealous and run to him for a kiss also.

After school, Bethie meets me at the bus stop.

"I shocked you," she says. "I'm sorry."

Embarrased recalling it all, I turn away.

"Please," she begs. "Let's still be friends."

I turn back and see her worried expression, and I can't bear the idea of her being upset because of me when usually I'm the shadow enjoying her constant radiance.

"I'll always be your friend," I promise.

She immediately returns to her former glowing self and suggests, "Let's go to the movies."

"Yes, let's! The musical *My Fair Lady* is playing at The Regent."

"After, come spend the night at my house."

"I'll use the pay phone in the cafeteria to ask my mom. Are your parents going to be there?" She nods. "Well then, I think she'll let me stay over." A strange expression flashes over Bethie's face, then disappears.

"I hope I like the movie. Did you know it's adapted from Shaw's play *Pygmalion*? After I read it, I got interested in the science of speech like Professor Higgins."

"It's a musical. I like some of them, especially when the songs are like poetry."

After the movie, we have dinner at a counter in Woolworth's

and then go to Bethie's house, which is in a nice-looking neighborhood of red brick homes and green lawns in a better part of town
than where I live.

For a while, we play Scrabble with her dad. Of course, she
lays down seven letters in triple-word squares almost at the start
of each game and then again, thereby building up her score while
I watch in disbelief. Her dad seems proudly amused while both of
us do our best here and there on the board, but mostly, we just
open possibilities with our minor plays for Bethie to score more
and easily win.

I would be completely demoralized by my low scores, but I,
too, see the humor in her mental showmanship and feel proud of
her each time she puts down seven-letter words, scoring doubles
and triples and extra points.

"Oh, not again, Bethie," Mr. Hartung would say each time,
laughing, and once, "Must you always shine it on over us? Soon
we'll just give up and not play with you."

I giggle hearing her feign "Sorry, Dad. Sorry Carol," and throwing us her encouraging crumbs with "But you're both improving.
Look how your scores are getting closer to mine each time." She
sounds so sincere that we can't fault her, and we just keep playing
until we get tired of losing.

When finally we've completed a last game, we fold the board
away, and say goodnight to Mr. Hartung.

Then I ask Bethie, "Shall we find your mom and say goodnight
to her, too?"

"She goes to bed way early," Bethie says. "Always."

Upstairs in Bethie's bedroom, she hands me a pair of her pajamas. "Loose-fitting?" I ask hopefully. They are, and soon I'm climbing into one of her twin beds. We talk for a long time about *My Fair Lady* and then discuss other movies we've seen, stopping only when Bethie falls asleep during my praising of Judy Garland's performance in *Meet Me in Saint Louis,* a movie I'd seen three times.

After falling asleep, I suddenly awaken to a series of moaning sounds flooding the house. Immediately I think of the hurt animal I'd heard crying in pain outside our house on a summer night with the windows open. Molly and I had run out in front just as the moaning stopped, and we saw some neighbors leaning over a little brown dog lying in the middle of the road. Someone then told us that the poor creature was dead.

The cries I'm hearing now in Bethie's house stop for a few minutes and then start again. Maybe it's a dream, I'm thinking, and I get out of bed to wake myself up, hoping the sorrowful sounds disappear, but they continue.

I get back into bed, and I glance over at Bethie in the bed next to me to see if she's awake. Her eyes are open and staring up at the ceiling, but she doesn't speak when she turns and sees me looking at her. Instead, she quickly turns toward the opposite wall.

"Bethie, what is that?"

"My mother," she answers, her face still turned away.

"She's crying."

"Don't listen," she advises in a monotone.

"Bethie, go see what's wrong," I urge.

"It doesn't help," she says with so little emotion that a chill runs through me.

"It's getting louder. Please go see! Talk to her."

"It doesn't help," Bethie insists.

For a while the crying stops. When it starts again, I beg Bethie to go comfort her mother, but this time she doesn't answer. How can she be asleep, I wonder. Trying not to listen, I cover my head with the pillow, but I can still hear. Bethie says she can't help. Does she mean she's tried and now is tired of trying?

But why isn't Bethie's father there beside her mother, his deeper voice mingling with her weeping while attempting to comfort her? Has he given up also? Maybe her mother sent them away... beyond consoling, needing to be alone in order to let go of all the pain of losing her son.

But she must know that I hear her, I'm thinking. Is she crying out to me because they've given up? No, she must realize I wouldn't try to comfort her without Bethie. And even if I did, it probably wouldn't help and she'd just be embarrassed.

For a few minutes, I feel the relief of only an echo of her grief penetrating Bethie's bedroom walls. But then new sobs hang on a faint blur of words, overwhelming me with their sadness through the partly open door. "Oh, my own darling boy..."

Trying not to cry, I push my face into the pillow.

When early dawn light filters in through Bethie's white organdy bedroom curtains, I feel myself drifting and then slowly fading into something like a dream.

In the morning, Bethie and I, still in pajamas, sit in the Hartungs' cheerfully decorated kitchen while her mother fixes us pancakes and eggs as if what went on last night never happened, and still feeling tired, I wonder now if it's all really been just a dream.

Bethie and I sit eating our pancakes and talking about the movie we'd seen the day before while her mother stands at the stove making another batch of pancakes.

"We saw *My Fair Lady* yesterday after school," I tell her. "Have you seen it?" She shakes her head no. "Well, it's about a girl who is trained by a Professor Higgins to become an elegant lady. I really recommend you see it, Mrs. Hartung."

"She doesn't go to movies," Bethie reports.

"It's starring Audrey Hepburn. She's been nominated to win an Oscar for Best Actress."

"She might win," Bethie says, "but I'm not much into people singing and dancing their feelings. I think it's kind of corny, really."

"Not if you let yourself feel the music take you into the story. I liked the way Eliza stood up for herself even when she was poor and selling flowers on the street. She was smart. The movie showed how people are mostly the same, depending on..."

"Whether or not they're willing to change," Bethie adds. "Shaw thought some of us could, I guess. But most of the songs got boring, I thought."

"Yes," I agree. "Too repetitious."

With my plate now empty, I look forward to another helping, which Mrs. Hartung soon offers me.

When Bethie asks me to pass the butter, her animated face, framed by a lock of golden-red hair, looms in sharp contrast to her mother's, which is almost expressionless. Thin wisps of gray and red strands fall across her cheek as she looks down at the skillet of sizzling, round pancakes. *Was she once a happy, pretty girl, maybe even brilliant like Bethie?* It seems hard to believe she could be the mother of a girl like Bethie. Mrs. Hartung seems so soft-spoken and gentle, a total contrast to my mother. Strange that Bethie's mom has a strong, confident daughter while my harsh, abrasive mother has me. But Molly's a lot like Mom, and I know Mom's glad about that. Maybe our fathers had more influence.

"These pancakes are great, Mrs. Hartung." I reach into the serving dish for another helping and feel glad to see her smile.

When we get up to leave, I notice a picture of a young boy on the top shelf of an oak cabinet near the door. All dressed up and smiling as if comfortable with who's taking the picture, he resembles Bethie, even with his brushcut.

Giving his photo a closer look, I decide that it must have been taken in a studio like the one in Witherton's Department Store that Molly, Mom, and I once passed while shopping for school clothes. Molly had said to Mom that we ought to stop on the way out and get photographed, sounding hopeful even though she knew we couldn't afford it. But Mom didn't become angry with her for asking, as she would have been with me. Only Molly can ask and get a simple, "No, dear, not today."

Bethie sees I'm pondering the boy's picture and says flatly, "That's my mother's son. From her first marriage. Before I was born."

Mrs. Hartung's eyes are now fixed on Bethie and she frowns. Then she turns away from us and quickly exits the kitchen through a doorway on the other side of the room.

After she's gone, Bethie continues telling me about what

happened to her brother, this time saying his name.

"We used to play games together until Alex wanted to hurt me."

"What kind of games?"

"Oh, just pretending games in some of the books he showed me, like 'Naughty Girl' and 'Make Your Donkey Mind' stories. But that day, he said we couldn't pretend anymore because now he wanted to hurt me. When I told my parents, my dad decided to send him to his uncle, who is still alive and living in Paris. A few months later, Alex had a heart attack during exercises at some boarding school there, and he died."

"I'm so sorry, Bethie."

"Well, I'm not sorry. He wanted to hurt me." Lifting her chin, she closes her eyes tight, I guess to blot out thoughts.

While I gather my things to leave, Bethie continues, "My mother and Alex were hidden by neighbors during the Vel'd'hiv Roundup, carried out by the French police doing the Nazis' bidding. Alex's father was arrested and sent to Auschwitz to work, then he was murdered. Somehow his older brother survived."

"How awful and sad for your mom."

"Yes. For all of us."

By the summer of our junior year at La Mesa High, Bethie, only fifteen, has completed all the graduation requirement classes and is enrolled in French and Spanish conversation classes at Carter Adult School to prepare, she says, for trips to France and Mexico she's planning.

After Bethie's Spanish class begins, we sit under a big umbrella at the local swimming pool, and while we eat hot dogs and chips, I listen to her tell about her date with a fellow adult school student-who she's sleeping with at his place after class.

"I need the experience of someone experienced," she laughs, and I try to laugh too, but I'm worried. She's begun to dress like my sister Molly and her college friends, who wear tight sweaters stretched over their nipple-showing breasts. Bethie's skirts are even shorter than theirs and too narrow for normal sitting, and now she always wears brightly colored, dangling earrings and blue eyeliner. Her face, freckled and rosy, still makes her look like a little girl, but she has a very full figure for a girl of fifteen. Her new clothing really emphasizes her tiny waist and round hips. Often I notice a few of our male teachers watching her as she passes them in the halls between classes, their eyes trailing until she turns the corner.

Before going back into the pool for another swim, she describes her date with another guy, also a student.

"He reminds me of my father and is almost his same age." Startled, my mouth hangs open. I can't believe she would want to date someone who looks like her father. Mr. Hartung is a short, chubby man, bald on top, with the rest of his grey hair forming a skirt around his shiny smooth head. Maybe a lawyer like her dad, but it's still creepy.

"Almost his same age?"

"Yes. I've told you, Carol. Experience is everything. Especially with sex, lots of experience is good." I'm picturing Mr. Hartung dressed as he is whenever I see him, in khaki pants, a short-sleeved Hawaiian shirt, and loafers. It's impossible for me to imagine

Bethie on a date with a man who looks that way.

Swimming back and forth in the outside lane, I start day-dreaming a more exciting scenario in which the guy she dates is one of Mr. Hartung's trim young clients, who one day sees Bethie and asks her to accompany him to the theatre. She is surprised and hesitates, but her father overhears, and I imagine him saying, "Oh, go ahead, Bethie. You love the theatre," so she goes out with him.

At the pool again a few weeks later, Bethie tells me she still likes dating the guy almost as old as her father. This time I fantasize that her date looks like Mr. Carpentier, the manager at the bank where I go each month to deposit checks for my boss at *The Desert News*. Mr. Carpentier looks like a movie star. He's tall, distinguished, with slightly greying hair carefully combed to look youthful. He's trim and always dressed in stylish, expensive-looking dark suits. *Maybe a man like him.* Suddenly, in my mind, Mr. Carpentier becomes an exciting, possible choice, stirring in me now strange, new thoughts and unsettling feelings.

"Bethie, aren't you afraid of getting pregnant?"

"I know how to take care of myself. Do you want to know how? I'll tell you."

"No," I answer quickly, afraid she might tell me something wrong and someday I'll get in trouble. Besides, I don't even have a boyfriend or expect to have one. I've already decided that my broad shoulders, narrow hips, and hardly noticeable waistline are too ordinary to attract the good-looking seniors I'd want to date. Plain dark hair and brown eyes seem no match for all the true and bleached blondes roaming our high school halls dressed in the latest fashions my family can't afford, even for Molly. I'm lucky to be able to fit into her hand-me-downs.

More than not wanting to hear the instructions on birth control Bethie offers, I don't want to hear what she might reveal about herself--the really intimate details, and I certainly don't want to hear more about anyone Bethie is sleeping with who reminds her of her father. Still, I've made up my mind to see only the best in her since that's how she sees me, and I'm committed to that and to believing it will go on forever. *I'll always be your friend.*

Toward the end of the summer, Bethie decides that we both must go to a top university together. I'll need to win a scholarship to make that happen. Bethie, however, has a straight-A grade-point-average along with a balanced extracurricular program, ensuring her a fully paid scholarship to three outstanding universities. She's chosen the University of Chicago.

"That's where all the real action is," she explains, "and where the professors write the texts used everywhere else. They're publishing and also teaching their undergraduates. That's for me, Carol. Even as a freshman, I want that kind of scholarly interaction."

Unlike Bethie, I have little interest in math or science, so I have high grades only in English and social sciences. I just have a B+ average, and what I earn after school at *The Desert News* goes for essentials and a little spending money, so I am limited to only a few extracurricular school activities. Therefore, my college plans hang on thin threads, one of which I may soon feel compelled to cut.

Our journalism teacher, Mr. Wanewright, hands us a list of

thirty high school newspapers and says with authority, "Memorize them for a test on Monday."

I guess for him it's some sort of exercise, like running laps, but for the first time in my high school career, I'm so outraged by the stupidity of an assignment that I become physically ill by lunch time. As we walk over to our usual lunch spot, Bethie realizes something is wrong with me when I run and vomit into a bush along the side of the quad.

When I'm feeling better, we sit together on a stairway nearby and she tries to comfort me while I complain bitterly about the upcoming test.

"I won't do it. I just can't. It makes me sick to even try."

"You don't have to do it," she reminds me.

"But I'll lose a chance for a scholarship if I don't get Wainwright's 'A'."

"It's not worth it for you. I'd memorize it just to get what I want, but I don't get sick or hate myself for doing that."

"Why not?" I ask, admiring her honesty.

"It's all a game to me, and I'm winning. Remember I told you I play only C's on the violin in orchestra for extracurricular credits toward winning a scholarship?"

I don't memorize the list of high school newspapers, my grade falls to a 'B', and I don't maintain the required grade-point-average to win a scholarship.

I'm devastated.

My parents don't understand my depressed state, and it upsets them since, taking their cues from outside sources, they believe my ambitions are unreasonable.

"Girls don't need fancy colleges," my mother declares.

"Be thankful, Carol, that you'll be able to go to City College right here in town," advises my always thankful father, and I think I should be, but I'm not.

"It's good enough. You always try to push yourself where you don't belong," my mother accuses. "Stop putting on airs or you'll end up nowhere," she warns.

Bethie helps me regain my self-respect and keep my dream of going to a major university. I keep thinking that she, a Jewish girl-genius, continues to have faith in me even though I've failed to distinguish myself in any way.

"I have a plan for you," she announces, opening her lunch bag and biting into half a sandwich. "By the way, where's your lunch?"

"I'm never eating again." She laughs but I don't.

"Hey, hear my plan before you decide to starve yourself."

"I'm listening."

"You'll be joining me at the University of Chicago only one year later."

I'm speechless as she writes a prescription for me. "Go to City College for one year, where you'll easily get excellent grades. Apply, concurrently, for admittance to the University of Chicago. I'm certain you'll pass their entrance exam, and when they see your excellent City College record, they'll offer you at least a fellowship. I'll help you find a part-time job as soon as you come to Chicago. We'll be dorm roommates! It'll be wonderful!"

"I don't belong there. I'm not smart enough."

"Yes, you *do* belong there," she insists.

"How do you know?" I want so much to believe her.

"You're smart...plus you have what Tillich calls rare moral courage. He says those who have it are able to know when the most essential aspects of life must prevail against whatever is less important. You have it! I've never seen that in anyone our age except you. In a way, you're kind of a moral genius."

I shake my head in disbelief.

"Here, I'll prove it to you." She tears out a sheet of blank paper from her notebook and writes three words on it...*knife, gun, club.*

I watch with hypnotic interest.

"Now you must choose one. If you were ordered to kill someone, which of these three weapons would you decide to use? Take your time. You have sixty seconds to respond."

A moment later, "Time's up. What did you choose?"

"I don't want to choose. I won't! I just wouldn't ever choose."

"See! That's the proof, right there. Everyone I have tested so far has always chosen...everyone except you. I would probably have to test hundreds more people to find another response like yours. I, myself, would have insisted on a fourth choice, maybe poison. Less messy. You know me, I always challenge orders. Hey, I guess you did too this time, didn't you?" She laughs to see I manage a smile, my first in a long while.

When she finishes her lunch, she takes out a chocolate bar and offers to share. When I shake my head, she asks, "How come you don't want any?"

"I like chocolate, but Molly says it'll make me fat."

"What does she know? I have a few bars every week and look at me. Am I fat?" She's very trim. She leans forward and almost whispers, "What's forbidden is so delicious, Carol, that always wanting it can make you sick."

"Okay, then give me some. I'm starving." She gives me the rest of her chocolate.

I'm beginning to realize now how much I love Bethie.

PART II

"Reaching Into the Storm"

EIGHT

"**W**hat's wrong with the kids?" Mark asks, coming home from work early and finding the baby crying in his crib and Daniel and Wendy fighting about something in the kitchen. He finds me in our bedroom, sitting amid yellowed copies of the letters Bethie and I had written to *The Chicago Tribune* spread all over the bed.

Hearing anger in his voice, I answer defensively, "Nothing's wrong with them. They're clean and fed."

"Is that enough? What's wrong? You were always such a perfect mother. And nothing's happening between us anymore. What's happened to my perfect little wife?"

A heavy silence. *Between us everything is only your way. Even our sex life. I dress up for you, say the words that turn you on and repeat them until I finish pleasing you, then put the pink slip, garter belt, and the silk stockings you insist I wear back into my drawer.*

"Well, Carol, what about it?"

Gathering the old letters and clippings into a pile, I lie down on the bed and turn away without answering.

"What's wrong with you, and what are you planning to do about it?" he wants to know.

"Maybe I should see Jenna's therapist."

"That's expensive."

"Mark, you said that something's wrong with me."

Turning me toward him and taking me into his arms, he whispers in my ear, "I'm missing you so much."

The rest of the day, I'm crying a lot and Mark keeps saying it's going to be okay, that I'll feel better soon, but I don't believe him. Bethie is dead. I'll never see her again. That's never going to be okay.

The next morning it is Mark's idea that I call to make an appointment to see Dr. Kelly. When, for the first time, he fixes breakfast for the kids and gets them ready for school, I know he really believes I need help, which scares me into making the phone call for an appointment, though I'm still half-hoping there'll be a long wait and I'll feel better soon and cancel.

"You're lucky," the receptionist says. "I can fit you in this afternoon at two o'clock."

Dr. Kelly's office is located just north of downtown Irvine. Jenna gave me directions and then drew me a map and brought it over before I left. She was worried that I'd get lost. She was probably right.

Leaving the comfort of our small university community, I feel even more upset as I pass by the campus on my way to the freeway and eye the students going to and from the main entrance. How often I hear a university called a city within a city, when really it isn't. Instead, it's more like a privileged sanctuary, inhabited mainly by carefree students, professors with jobs secured by tenure, and with a variety of supportive, paid student assistants, everyone covered by good health plans and with lots of vacations.

As I drive along the main street of the campus lined with tall buildings and giant trees, I long to be part of all that again. I want to park and visit the bookstore's coffee shop for a quick cup and then browse through the shelves in the poetry section to see the names of the fortunate few who managed to get published.

I push myself to drive on to the dreaded appointment, remembering Jenna's advice to think of Dr. Kelly as a kind of paid friend. A modern concept, I think. Someday it might become an everyday necessity for many of us. Certainly friendship will always be important enough to be fully exploited.

While heading for the freeway entrance, I imagine that in the future, one might buy a counseling program, something like those on the new teaching machines, have it in the home to turn on and be able to see a picture of someone's Dr. Kelly; another click might give detailed information about his background, qualifications, success record, etc.... How nice it might be to learn, in the privacy of our homes, his orientation--married, divorced, children, no children, pets, religious preference (or none), educational background, awards, no awards--so that if a Dr. Kelly cuts into our souls, we'll have the means to respond with some level of personal assault.

These ideas stumble through my mind as I take the University Street exit onto the 91 freeway and, as Jenna directed, go north toward the Riverdale Mall. I then take the turnoff onto Clover

Boulevard, and soon after making an immediate right onto Pearl Street, find a four-story office building which, I suspect, houses many of Jenna's "paid friends."

I had spoken with Dr. Kelly for only a few moments, telling him hesitantly about Bethie's letter and my upsetting phone conversation with her aunt, when he asks, "Why did your friend kill herself?"

His choice of words jabs me and I want to leave.

"Why couldn't you kindly say that she passed away?" I ask angrily, but he just smiles and jots something down on a clipboard with a yellow pad.

Dr. Kelly is a tall, slender, grey-haired man. He's wearing a sporty looking, casual outfit, probably to relax his patients, but it doesn't work for me. I sit across from him with my neck and shoulders locked in painful stiffness while he's writing something on his yellow pad. Probably noting my discomfort. *Why did I come? How can he help me?*

"She *did* kill herself, didn't she?" he questions.

When I don't answer, he continues, "Isn't that what you meant when you told me that you had lost a friend who suddenly ended her own life?"

LOST--the word stays in the air, so precisely does it speak of both Bethie and me. Will he refuse to continue, tell me to leave if I don't respond? I open my lips, but no words come. My eyes flood and I grab my purse and frantically search through several zippered pockets to find a tissue. Dr. Kelly, professionally prepared for tears, hands me the box of tissues on his desk.

"Your friend must have meant a lot to you, and now she's gone. She committed suicide, didn't she?"

"She committed…" I whisper. "Ended her…"

"Killed herself."

"Yes!" I shout at him. "She killed herself!"

"Do you know why?" When I shake my head no, he continues prodding. "Do you want to know? Or would you like to just accept it as a sad event, a loss, and go on with your life?"

"I don't seem to have that choice."

"Think about that feeling of helplessness." A long silence. Then, "Was your friend into drugs?"

"No. She always said people who used drugs might be messing up their minds permanently."

Another long silence while he wrote more, and then he challenged with, "Do you want to know but you're afraid of what you might learn?" I shrugged that off, but he wouldn't let go. "Well, in any case, now is the time to choose what you really want to do."

I want to take a happiness pill. I want to cry. I want to turn back time and walk the halls of La Mesa High, sit in the quad at Chicago with Bethie and discuss Plato. I want to "pass away" to somewhere else as quietly and gently as possible. I don't want to tell him any of this.

"She was very brave," I finally managed to say.

"I don't think so," Dr. Kelly responds.

"A lot braver than I am," I insist.

"Would you like to tell me more about that?"

I shake my head no, and we just sit quietly for the rest of the hour--a new kind of silence, which seems to be pointless, unnatural, and certainly expensive.

Before the session ends, Dr. Kelly suggests that I attend one of his group therapy sessions.

"No thanks! I'm afraid of groups. People in groups aren't predictable. I don't trust them."

"Being a member of one might help you, Carol," he says. "When situations and people must be predictable, it usually means a need for too much control."

"What's wrong with control?" *Never let anyone else decide your life. Don't let anyone mess with your mind.*

Dr. Kelly continues to advise, "If you need control too much, it may be impossible for you to get in touch with your true feelings about your friend and her death. What was her name again?"

"Elizabeth!" I hear myself call Bethie that for the first time, and somehow it gives me just enough control for a few more minutes to get myself out of there before I know I will be sick, and I head for the nearest restroom.

Once home, I replay my session with Dr. Kelly. How wrong he seems about Bethie. She *was* brave. I'm certain about that. Why then did she end her life? *I'll know when....* If only I knew why she chose that day. If it was somehow connected to an incident in the past, I might be able to understand why she decided it was time.

Searching for clues, my mind travels back to when we were together in Chicago.

NINE

After graduating from La Mesa High, Bethie and I move onto our differing paths in accord with her plan. We write to each other regularly, and she always includes words of encouragement along with explanations of the admissions process, which I follow to the letter and mail out my application.

Sometimes she shares her detailed descriptions of college events, but I can't tell from them if she's happy there. She does say that even though she misses me, she's glad to have left our town and classmates.

During her first quarter at Chicago, she's given a series of tests, and with her high scores, she passes out of two years of general education requirements. She's sixteen years old and already considered a third year student at Chicago, while I'm attending the local community college, studying hard and working part-time.

In March, I receive a letter confirming that I've been accepted at the University of Chicago and awarded a fellowship, which will cover my tuition during the four years as an interest-free loan I can pay back gradually after I graduate. It's more than I expected, and I begin to believe, along with Bethie, that I may actually be someone special, a need that I can recall having taken root in me long before I met Bethie.

* * *

I am six years old. Mom is in the kitchen, busy making challah, a braided bread for our Sabbath meal. I join her there at the table to watch, and she gives me a large chunk of dough to make my own small loaf.

As Mom instructs, I separate it into three equal parts and roll each one into a strand long enough to braid. Next, I pinch the stretched strands together at their tops and braid them the way I did my pigtails each morning while wishing my hair was thicker like Molly's.

Mom smiles at my little loaf and carefully lays it on the pan next to hers, then puts them into the oven. While I watch her wash the mixing bowls, I ask her the question on my mind since my second week in the first grade at Lincoln School when the teacher had moved me from the Redbird group, reading in the red books, to the Grasshopper group, in the green books.

Everybody thinks the Grasshoppers are the smartest, best readers.

"Mom, am I smart?"

"Just average."

"What's average?"

"Nothing special."

"Who's special?"

"Your cousin Rachel. She skipped a grade."

"How about Molly?"

"She's especially pretty."

"I'm in the green book now," I announce proudly, "and I didn't even have to catch up."

Mom doesn't seem to hear me. She says she has to make a phone call and hurries out of the kitchen.

Not being special to Mom makes me feel sad.

Bethie is excited about my coming to Chicago. But when I bring up the idea of rooming together, she writes back, "I had a bad time with a roommate last fall, so I've requested a single." I'm disappointed but still happy to be joining her at Chicago and in the same dorm.

When I arrive on campus, even in autumn its great Gothic halls are still rich with green ivy coverings and trellises on Blair Hall, my assigned dorm, where I soon meet Margaret, my roommate. She lived at Blair last year, and as soon as she learns that I'm Bethie's friend, she makes it clear she wants nothing to do with her.

It seems Bethie's high school reputation has followed her here. When I question Margaret further, she describes Bethie as a shockingly peculiar female genius. She speaks of "last year's incident" in hushed tones, suggesting a very strange relationship between Bethie and her roommate. Apparently, the roommate, Allison Wayman, was heard crying most nights and had purchased a gun, which she showed to the two girls in the neighboring room. They reported it, and she was then asked to leave. Her parents were called and they came and took her home.

It seems to me that no one knows exactly what went on

between Bethie and Allison, but imaginations have swelled with the mystery. According to Margaret, "To everyone's surprise, Bethie continued to attend her classes as usual. She acted as if nothing happened."

Soon after settling in, I go to see Bethie. Her room is one of only two on the fifth floor, and she paid double to have it to herself. If the stories about her are true, maybe she's come to believe she's better off rooming alone.

We hug in the doorway, then look at each other.

"We're both prettier now," she says, smiling. "That's good. We're on our way!"

"Where to?" I ask, laughing.

"Everywhere. I can't wait to leave!"

"I just got here."

"Well, come on in. See my little cage."

A quick scan of the room at first gave it a sense of normalcy for a dorm; two of everything--beds, dressers, desks, chairs and closets--identical with our rooms below. The shock comes when I glance at the hanging blanket tacked up over her bed. It has a swastika woven into the center.

"What's the swastika for?" I ask, trying not to look at it, but then I can't help staring at it again.

"Scary, huh? And you know why? Because it's a symbolic reminder of the Jewish children like us burning in Hitler's ovens. Kids, like us, Carol." She stands there watching me hug myself while trying to keep that hardly believable terror from revisiting my mind.

I'd first heard about the Holocaust in Sunday School twelve years after the war ended. My father had never spoken of it to us, probably wanting to spare Molly and me from knowing about all those whom the God he loved could not save. I look away, chilled even more by that thought, and Bethie sees that and says, "I keep looking at it so it won't ever scare me again. It's an effective psychological technique I've learned. It works for me."

On another wall, she's hung a picture of a gun cabinet with one gun obviously missing. On one of the desks there's a statue of two naked bodies so entwined that I can hardly tell them apart. Looking closer, I see lines of rope around their necks. They appear to be standing on a scaffold together, about to be hanged. I wonder if this is what Bethie creates to keep herself going. She's always needed psychological risks, once insisting that a startled brain is like a car being jump started to get it working. However, in just these few minutes I've spent in her room, I'm overwhelmed by ugliness all around.

"Carol, my dad says we're all survivors of that war--those who lived, made it to America, and even their children."

"Like you and Alex?"

"Especially Alex. He had to live with the loss of his real father and our mother's grief and depression."

Bethie now focuses her attention on a box sitting on a table near her bed, and soon she pulls out a small metal pot with a plug in its side. "Tea time," she calls out, filling the pot with water and plugging it in.

On her other bedside table, I recognize a pile of books from the list I saw posted for OMP (Organization, Methods, and

Principles of Knowledge), a required course for seniors in the Liberal Arts College.

"How come you're reading for OMP this year?" I ask.

"I'm a senior now." Seeing my obvious surprise, she explains, "I passed out of the rest of the general ed requirements by exam. No use to waste time in classes. I've got more important things to do."

She responds to my puzzled look with, "I told you, I want to experience everything. And I'm never going to grow old, so I have to hurry." Soon she offers me some tea. It tastes bitter and grainy.

"What is this stuff?" I ask, sipping slowly while my eyes cautiously move over the posters on the walls. I'm trying not to react overtly to them, not wanting to feel manipulated into showing alarm.

"I don't know anything about this tea," she says. "A funny old guy I met at the open market gave me some."

I cough and spill the rest into her plastic-lined trash can. "It could be anything, Bethie, anything."

She falls across her bed laughing at me.

"Sometimes I think you're crazy," I say in earnest, watching her sit up then and drink the rest of that tea.

"I know, everyone does. But I'm not. I'm just really different--smarter and braver than most people."

"Take down the swastika," I shout at her, "or I'm leaving and not coming up here again."

She pulls the blanket off the wall and throws it in the corner.

Before leaving for the bookstore, I ask Bethie about her room-mate last year. She calmly answers, "Allison's a very disturbed girl. I'm glad she left."

I wait for more details. A pause. Then she tells me, "You won't believe this, Carol, but she was extremely jealous of the man I was also sleeping with at the time." Having already heard many stories about Bethie and her roommate, I'm having no trouble believing it.

Since Bethie occupies the single room just above ours, Margaret keeps pointing out many of Bethie's strange habits. "She's pacing again," Margaret often says, annoyed and disgusted. Sometimes Bethie paces for hours. The walls and ceiling are thin, so we know exactly where and when. I don't know which bothers me most, the pacing or Margaret's angry complaints, so I bring it up the next time I see Bethie to let her know her pacing disturbs us. She just smiles at me, a little embarrassed, but says nothing.

Soon after, Bethie buys an old rocking chair at a Goodwill Store, has it delivered up to her room, and the pacing is replaced by rocking. Often, during the designated study period in our dorm, she rocks the entire time. I mention this to her, and she responds that she does her best thinking and studying in her rocker. "It's also part of my thirty-minute meditation period. Carol, you can't imagine the insights this kind of thinking brings. Must be something about the brain I need to learn more about."

When I explain all this to Margaret, she says simply, "She's crazy."

It seems that rocking and craziness have long been associated. At least, I know that's how my mother saw it, and sometimes when I hear Bethie's rocker pressing in rhythm against our ceiling, it reminds me of the day when I first learned that my rocking frightened both of my parents, and especially my mother.

"Aaron, a four-year-old girl shouldn't sit and rock all day. Sophie's girl, too, like a dummy sits and rocks. Maybe Carol, God forbid, is retarded."

Daddy is angry. *"What kind of talk from you, Belle? Bite your tongue! What do you know...you all day with the cooking, cleaning, your stories on the radio? Not even to ever open a book! When I come home, she runs to me with her questions. She's got more sense than you."*

Now I hear Mommy crying, and then Daddy says, "If something's wrong, take her to a doctor. Find out!"

Mommy is still crying. Daddy made Mommy cry.

I rock with Dolly until her pretty blue eyes stay back in her head. "Oh, Dolly, I'm sorry."

Later, Mommy and I trudge up the hill in the snow. She's angry and worried. Her voice tells it all to me earlier during lunch before we leave. "Sit still and eat. Don't play with it. Stop talking and eat! We have to go see the doctor." The radio voices drone on. A nap first with no-eyes-now Dolly. I sing to her, "Rock with me, Dolly, rock, rock."

At the top of the hill we go into the building made of big red blocks. Then in the big room with the sun peeking in the window over a table of toys, a tall man speaks to me nicely. Like Daddy!

"What do you see here, Carol?"

"Light dancing in pieces on the window."

"What else, Carol?"

"All colored cups there...a blue, a red, green one."

"Would you like to hold this doll?"

"Oh, she has her eyes. My dolly's are gone."

I take the doll into another room, but I can still hear my mother talk to the doctor who plays with me.

"What's wrong with her, Doctor?"

"Nothing, Mrs. Mandell. She's a bright little girl. She just needs someone to play with."

"What should I do? Stand on my head?"

"How about nursery school?"

"We can't afford that."

"I'll help you get her in somewhere."

On the way back down the hill, Mommy holds my hand, not pressing so hard. "At least you're not a dummy like Sophie's girl. Sits and rocks all day and she's seven years old. No more rocking, you hear me, Carol? Soon you'll be a schoolgirl like Molly."

"I'll be like Molly," I nod, smiling. "A schoolgirl."

I guess I must have stopped rocking, and I remember loving the nursery school. Maybe Bethie's mother didn't ever imagine her being a dummy.

Actually, I'm not as worried about Bethie's proclivity for pacing and rocking as about the older men who visit her in the dorm lounge. She usually leaves with one of them and doesn't return until very late. I try to stay up until I hear her footsteps above us.

TEN

Just before Christmas vacation, Bethie suggests I help her select a tree for her room. "I know you don't celebrate Christmas, but I do." Laughing at my surprised look, she says, "It's fun, and essential to our economy. Why not enjoy it?"

"I enjoy Thanksgiving."

I search for a place to sit among her layers of clothes and books and find a small vacant area at the head of her bed. I plop down. "The whole season from then on depresses me."

"Hmm. Puzzling. Why?" She settles in her rocker on top of what seemed like a mountain of clean but very wrinkled laundry.

"I feel like an American except at Christmas. That's how it is for me," I answer, but I know there's more to it, and I soon find myself relating the traumatic incident I'd experienced as a little girl just before Christmas.

"We lived in Utica, New York, then, in a neighborhood of mostly poor, immigrant families, all of us crowded into old, run-down apartments housing people from many different backgrounds, but all of us were very proud to be Americans living in 'the land of the free and the brave.'

"As Jewish kids, we were expected to wear two heavy and

sometimes uncomfortable hats at the same time.

"And, as it was written: Thou shalt not covet thy neighbor's... 'Yes, God,' I confessed, 'I carry my tree home every year in my heart, decorate it with too many lights.' Unbalanced by the glitter and the gorgeous window displays downtown, I went blindly into the madness of it all.

"At home, we had our own holidays, too. Little gifts and treats from my grandmother wearing her faded, long-sleeved dresses, all reminders to me of her past suffering in what she called 'the old country.' And, of course, Hanukah didn't glitter in the streets like Christmas. Christmas, with its putting of dreams under branches, is everywhere from Thanksgiving to New Year's...in windows, on rooftops, at school, stores. Christmas, with its snow-white charity and love, was everywhere I went... except that one day just before Christmas....

"I was on my way home from school when I saw them come across the street, all five in my third grade class. One shouted, 'Dirty Jesus-killer!' Then they surrounded me chanting, 'Dirty Jew, that's you, a dirty Jew.'

" 'I didn't,' I screamed, but they continued chanting while pulling at my jacket and hood. Then one grabbed my books and threw them into the snow. When I bent to pick them up, another kid pushed me back down and kept kicking me until a lady, just then passing by, made him stop.

" 'What are you doing? Shame on you!' the lady yelled. 'I'm going to call the police. They'll come after you and lock you up for Christmas.'

"They all ran, and she helped me up and wiped my face with

her scarf. 'They're gone,' she said. 'I scared them plenty, Honey. They won't bother you any more.'

"It turned out she was right. In January, when we went back to school, all the kids involved seemed to have forgotten what happened. Except me, of course, whose child heart had been purged of its sin. Never again would I ever dare envy their Christmas.

"And after that," I tell Bethie, patiently listening to my traumatic holiday saga, "Christmas has never been the same."

"No wonder you get depressed," she says. "So let's erase it with some fun today. Okay? Let's go to Little Italy on the IC train. I have an old friend downtown who makes great pizza at a little restaurant there."

Bethie's friend turns out to be an older guy, or so he seems to me, and their easy familiarity indicates more than just a casual friendship. But I don't ask Bethie for details. I'm afraid to hear what she might tell me.

We spend many lazy hours during Winter Break in her single room at our dorm enjoying the comfort of her rocker with me stretched out on her bed while her tiny Christmas tree lights flicker on and off, and I listen to the excursions of her notorious, brilliant mind.

Sometimes she tries her best to involve me in her ongoing mathematical speculations:

"Carol, just think, as early as the end of the 19th century, it was proved that the way prime numbers are distributed is in a simple pattern. The average spacing between primes near a number x is *that* x's natural logarithm. Amazing, huh?"

"Sure. Amazing." My head's spinning. "What else is new in

the x world?"

Realizing I've disconnected, Bethie moves on to something else.

"Okay. Let's talk about philosophy. Or better yet, how about magic realism?"

"What's that?"

"You know. Like when a writer creates an illusion... narrates the inexplicable, ignoring the rules of nature."

"Oh, yes." I'm excited now for our conversation to continue. "Like events taking place in an ordinary world that might seem unreal but are perceived as normal."

"That's it."

"Like when characters talk to their dead relatives."

Bethie's eyes well up with tears, and I immediately regret my example.

"I might try that," she replies almost in a whisper, and that conversation ends.

Later that afternoon, Bethie tells me again about the train ride home from her brother's funeral and how her father's simple words "now you are all we have" inspired and energized her to seek greater and greater achievements.

"I knew before I could tie my own shoes," Bethie explains, rocking faster, "that my mind had unusual powers. My dad just helped me focus them. He would play number games with me. When we played store, I'd end up teaching him how to make change in four different number systems. What fun to see him so excited and proud."

"He must have been amazed!"

"At first, I guess. But soon he decided to expand my curriculum to include languages. French and German for starters. While he continued to talk to me in German most of the time at home, he hired his friend, Mr. Mallencoff, to teach me Russian after school. I'd already picked up Spanish from Anita, the lady who cleaned our house each week, and I'd started doing all my school reports in at least two other languages, clipping them together. English on top, of course."

"What did your teachers think?"

"Most didn't like me. I thought they were dumb, and they knew it."

I imagine them trying to handle this wonder child, struggling to challenge her or at least keep her busy. But, like all children, Bethie must have wanted their approval. *Does she ever hate the climb to where her father waits to assign her more and more challenges?*

As if anticipating my question, she announces, "My father is my mentor and I love him for that."

Maybe with each easily won achievement, does he lift her from loneliness to another new high? And how does Bethie's mother fit into all this?

"Your mother must have been so upset when your brother died," I say, pressing to understand more. She turns away for a moment without answering, then continues our conversation by changing the subject and suggesting, "Why don't we do something exciting? Let's go to the anti-war rally. I hear there's a plan to take over the Administration Building. Also, I want to join the protest march on Washington. Will you go with me?"

"No. I'm afraid to go. With crowds of angry people, anything can happen," I warn. "We might end up in jail!"

"That would be great! Important! I want to be part of that. Help make history. Come with me!"

"I can't. I'll write something for the newspaper."

I know I'm letting her down, but I just can't go.

Bethie went alone and reported back to me, "Nothing bad or good happened. It was just a waste of my time."

"What about history?"

"Maybe if I go to Berkeley, where the *real* action is. Mario Savio said it right. We have to put our bodies on the line in any real struggle."

Somehow I convince Bethie not to go to Berkeley. Instead, we send letter after letter to the *Chicago Tribune* in support of free speech and civil rights, against the Vietnam War and against the draft, and the *Tribune* prints several of Bethie's letters and a few of mine. Then a reporter from *The Maroon,* our college press, writes about our letters in the *Tribune,* including some excerpts, and for a while we're famous on campus.

Our dorm throws a party for us. Someone pours champagne and Bethie offers a toast as we all lift our glasses: "To peace that will eventually come when we're all dark-skinned and admit we're bisexual."

Several glasses lower.

"Well, that's when peace will happen," she explains after noticing how many have become less enthusiastic.

Standing to one side, I wait, anxious for it to be over, but she goes on speaking about us someday having rights that most of us can't imagine we'll ever want.

"The freedom to love anybody, everybody, openly," she exclaims. "What we need is more love, not less."

Many seem to be agreeing with that last point, but, as always, she feels compelled to go beyond, advocating some benefits of interracial marriages. "Yes, it's even healthier. So why not? Someday, we'll all look the same. That means less hate and less war." A lot of groaning and shuffling then, and many leave before we cut the celebration cake. A few stay, and one guy, the only one wearing a business suit, shakes her hand.

The next day a full report of her speech at our celebration appears in the *Tribune*, likely written by the guy in the suit.

Did she make history? In a way, I suppose. But what I remember most of that evening is Bethie's decision to actually contribute financially someday toward her dream of a more just world with equal opportunity for all.

"When I have some money of my own, I'm going to give two scholarships to the university, one for an annual poetry prize for women students and one covering tuition for a black student. Have you noticed how few of them are around here?" I haven't, I'm ashamed to say.

"Do you plan to have enough money to do that?"

"Yes. I have an inheritance coming from my paternal grandmother when I graduate."

"I didn't know she died. When was that?"

"When I was gone that whole week in high school."

"You never said."

"She'd been sick for a long time in some nursing home in New York. I didn't even know her. My dad took her death hard though. I went with him to see her. She died the next day."

"How sad. Mark's grandmother died in a nursing home too. She lived with his family for most of his life, and they were close."

"Mark? Oh, that guy you dated that writes plays. You're still dating him. Great!" She sounds too happy. I'm suspicious. "It's about time, Carol?"

"For what?"

"Your sex life to begin, of course."

My cheeks burn while she continues, "You're on your way now." How long has she been waiting--and for what? I frown and punch her right shoulder, one step beyond silence.

"Hey!" she laughs. "Okay, kiddy, I'll stop, but I'd like to meet Mark. What's his major?"

"He's in third-year science classes mainly, though he likes literature and philosophy more. Right now he's reading the Binyon translation of Dante's *The Divine Comedy*."

"Oh, I've read Michele Barbi's article on Dante in the *Enciclopedia Italiana*. We'll have a lot to talk about."

I tell Mark about Bethie and that she wants to meet him, and he teases, "Okay, Carol, I'll meet your genius friend, but I'm warning you. I'm very attracted to smart women. Like you," he adds. To be kind, I am thinking.

I laugh. "Like me? I can't wait to see you two talking up a storm about Dante. It'll be fun. Just don't drink the tea in her room if she offers it."

Of course, I don't confess that I hope he doesn't like her too much. She attracts all eyes when we go places. Why not Mark's? And what could be worse than your best friend seriously attracting your boyfriend away? But it's inevitable that they meet, so I'll plan to set the stage and be ready for whatever happens.

"Wait a minute," he says. "Is your friend Bethie the Elizabeth Hartung taking OMP?"

"Yes. I saw her OMP books on her desk. She's taking it."

"Okay, then I know who she is. Wow. She runs our professor in circles translating from the originals. She quotes whole pages of our required readings from memory. Makes everyone feel dumb, including Professor Bindman."

"Well, anyway, do you still want to meet with her?"

"Yes, but not to discuss Dante. And let's do it soon, before Christmas vacation ends and our classes start again."

Mark and I meet Bethie at a pizza place near the campus. A few days earlier, she'd mentioned that she had a date with someone who would be meeting her there at eight o'clock. When I'd suggested that Mark and I could meet her there earlier, she'd said that was a great idea, that Mark and she could get acquainted and even have time to talk about Dante. I'd just said okay. I didn't tell her Mark didn't want to talk with her about Dante. I decided to let things happen naturally.

At the pizza parlor, right from the start Bethie and Mark don't hit it off. He speaks in a guarded way and Bethie jumps on his every pronouncement like some *New York Times* literary critic. We drink beer and call to the people we know who come and go. Then Bethie starts to flirt with Mark. I hate her for that! Half-drunk, she leans on his arm, smiling, and whispers something. He grimaces, then looks over at me and turns away, leaning against the back of his chair while finishing his beer. At that moment, he looks even more appealing to me than ever, his beige suede jacket zipped open halfway, showing his bare muscular chest covered with a thin layer of curls. Even frowning, he's terribly handsome.

I wonder what just happened between them, but I don't ask and stop hating her. I'm just glad Mark doesn't seem attracted to her even though she's so beautiful.

"She comes on too strong," he tells me when we're on our way to the movies.

"What's wrong with being strong?" I ask.

"Too strong isn't good, Carol. Not for a girl." We stop at the corner and he kisses me and says, "But you're perfect." I try to believe this is truly a compliment, although something about it now hurts. But then, I used to think kissing on street corners looked stupid, but today it seems quite wonderful.

Bethie and I meet at the campus bookstore, and longing to know her thoughts about Mark, I ask, "How come Mark and you didn't talk about Dante last evening?" I'm wondering about their whispering but don't plan to mention that unless she does.

"When I drink beer, Dante just falls away."

We both laugh.

"I recognized him from OMP class. He's very handsome, Carol. You make a great couple."

I start to ask about their whispering, but she stops short in front of a bench occupied by two small birds with pointed bills and colorful plumage, and when they quickly fly off, we sit down in their places and she tells me, "Those so-called sparrows are really finches of the Emberizidae family, seed-eaters and very gregarious."

"Uh-huh. I guess you've studied them, right?"

"Yes. Fascinating how we're so much like birds."

"I don't see that," I admit.

"Well, our arms are like wings, and our early ancestors might have copied singing, and then extended that into speaking words."

I love hearing her talk that way. She opens my mind to the natural world. Of course, she's studied Darwin. But, unlike him, she doesn't worry about some contradictions between his studies and the Bible.

ELEVEN

As soon as Bethie's father is willing to pay her rent, she moves out of the dorm and into a tiny apartment four blocks away. This is a short time before the popular Beatles songs like *Eleanor Rigby* poured their beautiful, alarming messages into young, solitary hearts like mine.

I'm working hard now on my studies each night and attending classes all day, then going to my job every afternoon, sometimes even on weekends. I don't have much of a social life, so when the song becomes popular, I can easily identify with all those lonely people they sing about.

Bethie, however, never seems to be lonely.

When I walk by her place to and from the job that she found for me with The News Express, a South Side neighborhood weekly, I sometimes see a man coming or going. All her male admirers look odd to me, but I've come to expect that since she isn't ordinary either. Once I asked her about someone I'd seen with her, but she just smiled and changed the subject, so I stopped asking.

Around sunset, when I arrive at her door for dinner, I meet a dark-haired, ragged-looking, very slim fellow there. He has a large, gray and white shepherd dog with him. Even though it's a chilly late fall evening, he's wearing sandals, walking shorts and a thin faded yellow shirt. Both he and I seem surprised to discover we'd both been invited. After I knock, he pulls out a key and smiles.

Bethie greets us at her door, and then she insists that the dog be kept out on the step "this time." *For my benefit? Okay other times?*

I soon learn that her friend, whom she introduces by first name only as Tarik, has been a graduate student for four years but is now thinking about going back to Pakistan soon without a degree since his parents have chosen a bride for him.

We eat sitting on the floor with our legs crossed. The food tastes remarkably good, but Bethie still has to explain most of it to me so I'll know what I'm eating. Maybe they're Tarik's favorites.

I'm enjoying the evening of talk and interesting food until Tarik and Bethie begin to kiss passionately. They don't seem to mind that I'm there, but I'm uncomfortable watching them, and when I quickly get up and give some excuse to leave, they don't seem to mind that either. I guess they're telling me it's okay, whatever I've decided.

The dog outside howls as I walk down Pine Street toward the dorms. Tarik, I'm sure, will stay on for a while, or maybe for the night, and invite the dog in now that I've left. Does Bethie care at all about Tarik's marriage plans? I suppose not since she didn't seem even a little surprised when he told us about them.

Unlike me, Bethie would never let anyone spoil her fun or change her plans. In fact, once she even saved me from changing mine, which would have been an academic disaster without her insight and encouragement.

During my first semester at the University of Chicago, I had a very humiliating experience with a woman professor, and I told Bethie that I wanted to drop out, but she insisted, "Don't let Wildenberg decide your future for you, Carol." At the time, I was sitting in Bethie's rocking chair and feeling grateful for its comforting motion though still feeling upset, and I described the incident exactly as it occurred that morning in my poetry seminar.

"Professor Wildenberg has asked us each to share our interpretation of William Blake's poem 'London'. When it's my turn, as I am speaking, she's looking at me and frowning. Then she's shaking her head and uttering very audible negative noises, so I speak more haltingly, losing confidence in what I'm saying. Still I try to continue giving my interpretation, and then I somehow manage to put forth the idea that Blake seems to me to be describing the state of powerlessness of the poor in an immoral, dark world.

"Interrupting me, Wildenberg shouts out, 'Stop right there.' She throws her book down on her desk, and says, 'I cannot believe, Miss Mandell, that you actually believe a great poet like Blake would have such simple-minded thoughts! Blake is clearly saying in this poem that marriage, not errant husbands, causes prostitution. He obviously implies that marriage as an institution caused the syphilis epidemic in London at that time.'

" 'You said not to read our own ideas into the work,' I remind her, and some of my fellow students giggle, I suppose enjoying the argument.

"Bethie, aren't differences of opinion expected at a great

university like Chicago where students are encouraged to express their ideas?"

"Yes, of course! Well, what did Wildenberg say after your challenge?"

"Wildenberg returns with, 'I suspect that everybody of literary merit interpreting the poem finds in it a clear indictment against religion and marriage.'

" 'That's not how I read it,' I persist, and I hear laughter coming from both sides of the room and angering her even more.

"Finally, she flaunts her authority, saying, 'I strongly suggest, Miss Mandell, that you read more deeply if you hope to pass this course.'

"I don't remember a single word of the discussion that followed. I just had to sit there and tell myself to freeze because I knew if I ran out, I'd really look like a fool."

"Good thinking," Bethie says. "Besides, several interpretations of that poem agree with yours, I recall. I'll hunt them up and you can show them to her."

"I don't ever want to go back into that classroom."

Bethie shakes her head in disapproval while I continue my lament. "I might as well just go home. The old crow'll probably give me a low grade, and I'll lose my fellowship, which means the end of college for me."

Hearing that, Bethie grabs me by the shoulders and looks straight into my wet eyes. "You have to stay, Carol. I challenge you to stay. Don't allow that bitch to decide your life! Don't let her mess with you."

"I'm already messed," I say, smiling into my tears.

"You're wonderful," Bethie exclaims with so much conviction that I begin to believe her. With motherly tenacity, she insists, "Promise me you won't leave, Carol, and I'll order us a pizza, the best…from Little Italy."

I promise, and that evening we eat pizza and drink beer until our stomachs ache. Secretly, I plan to attend but never speak again in Wildenberg's class and at least pass the course.

TWELVE

After Bethie moved out of the dorm, we saw each other much less often. Now she had the duties involved in apartment living along with a full schedule of senior level classes. When we talked on the phone, she would update me on the most general aspects of her very active sex life, like who she met where, when, and who else she was also seeing. Bethie did most of the talking since, by comparison, my life seemed rather ordinary even though, by then, I'd been dating Mark exclusively for almost a year, and our relationship steadily became more serious after the day we met at the college bookstore.

During my first week on campus, I'm standing in a long line waitng for my turn to buy my books. The lists of required reading for general education classes is enormous at Chicago, where many of our professors wrote the books for our classes, and they are used in classes all over the world.

While I watch a student walk by me carrying a pile of at least ten books, I overhear a girl in jeans and a big leather jacket being told her total comes to two hundred dollars. I gasp hearing that amount, then wonder what I'm facing as I step up to the now ominous sound of "Next."

After handing the student clerk my list of required books and waiting while she goes to gather them, I happen to turn and see a good-looking guy wearing a baseball cap in line behind me perusing his list. He glances up at me and smiles.

The clerk returns with books piled high on a rolling cart. After she rings up my books, she hands me a slip with the total.

"Two hundred and twenty, did you say?" I repeat in astonishment, "Two hundred and twenty?"

Mark, who is the guy under the baseball cap, hears and moves closer while the clerk nods, probably embarrassed for me as I stand here trying to handle the realization that I'm unable to pay the cost of the required books. My fellowship covers tuition, room and board, and what was designated as a small sum of money toward books. I naively assumed it would be enough, but now I know my account won't cover this until the end of the month when my father usually sends me a few extra dollars to add to what I earn at my part-time job.

If I can't do the reading assignments, I'm thinking, I might as well go home. I imagine myself trying to explain the situation to my parents.

The long line of students behind me waits as I search my over-filled purse for my checkbook in order to write the check that will surely bounce.

I'm half-turned to tell the guy in the baseball hat behind me I will step aside to write the check when he taps me on the shoulder and asks, "Can I see your list?"

Feeling helpless, I hand it to him.

He smiles at the clerk and glances over the titles.

"You don't need this one or this...or any of these now. I learned that last year." He points, "Just buy these and you'll be fine for the next few months." He checks them off quickly, then hands back the list, which I give to the clerk, saying I want only the checked ones for now. She's a little annoyed with me but adds up the new, shorter list.

I move to the side to write a non-delinquent check, grateful to the fellow with the timely advice. He moves up with his own list, and when the clerk leaves to gather his books, he introduces himself.

"I'm Mark Simon." He extends his hand. "You are?"

"Carol Mandell. I'm really grateful for your help."

After hearing my name, I like that he repeats it, as if addressing somebody important. "Well, Carol Mandell, how about some coffee when we're through here?"

"Yes. I certainly could use some."

While I wait for him to pay for his books, he tells me he is working on a play, and he then asks, "Could I read a few lines to you?"

"Of course. I owe you at least that much!"

We go to his favorite coffee shop off campus just a few blocks from the dorms, and over coffee and donuts, he reads me the first act of his play. It's about a blind music student who witnesses a murder.

"What a good plot idea," I say, impressed. "What's going to happen? Does the murderer see him as a threat?"

"I don't know yet."

"Now's the time to decide," I advise. "Murder mysteries require extensive planning."

He laughs and agrees. Then he asks if we could meet again soon to discuss it, since he hopes to finish it in time to submit to a South Side community theatre group who are looking for original scripts. I give him my phone number; however, he doesn't call until a few months later.

At first I'm annoyed when I hear him asking me for a date after I'd given up waiting, but when he explains that he has been laid up with a back injury acquired during a wrestling match, I eagerly accept his invitation to see the current opera at the Chicago Lyric. "I've got two rear balcony tickets to *Tosca,* and after, we can go eat somewhere nearby."

I'm thrilled with his plan. I love *Tosca* and dreamed of someday seeing it on stage.

Mark and I see a wonderful *Tosca*, and even with our seats far from the stage, we're able to observe all the highlights by sharing Mark's opera glasses.

After that evening, Mark and I date often. He reads me more parts of his play, and I tell him about my role in the Modern Dance Symposium at the end of the year.

"I've choreographed two dances for my class, and they'll soon be performed with me dancing the lead in one."

"No wonder you have that great body," he says, casting his eyes over me. "I'll go to the symposium. I want to see you dance."

I laugh. "Why not just take me dancing now?"

"Okay!"

We go dancing at Callaway's House of Music. After that, nearly every Saturday night, Mark picks me up at the dorm and we walk over to Jimmy's Tavern, a South Side hangout. When some of his friends are there with their dates, he proudly introduces me to them. They drag chairs from other tables to fit us in and buy us drinks. Then Mark buys a round. Before long we're all dancing to some great, local rock'n'roll bands.

Along with Jimmy's, there's The Compass, where Nichols and May are doing improvisation comedy. Some of us in the audience call out a few words, and they build a whole comedy scene using our prompts.

When Mark's play is in rehearsals, we drop in from time to time to watch. Mark likes hearing the director discuss it, and I'm curious how certain scenes work, particularly the ones I've helped him rewrite.

Opening night is exciting. During intermission, we stand at the refreshment bar in the lobby to overhear comments about the play. Mark worries, but it seems to me the audience likes it, and then most of the full house return to their seats, always a good sign.

In November, Mark comes to all my dance rehearsals and then to see me dance at the Symposium. He brings me a lovely bouquet of flowers at the conclusion. It scares me to feel like a princess in a story book even for a little while, but it helps to have Mark making it seem real.

Mark is the first guy I've dated who wants to talk as well as "make out." That combination, along with his trim build, silky black hair and romancing eyes, make him irresistible.

We soon discover that both of our families moved to Tucson, Arizona in the spring of 1960. Living on opposite sides of town, we'd gone to different high schools, and although we're both Jewish, we'd never met at religious events since Mark's parents are Temple Emanuel members whereas my parents belong to Beth Israel and each congregation had its own youth group. Now our stimulating late-night talks have quickly moved our relationship into wanting more intimacy, but we have nowhere to go to be alone together.

Then, one Saturday, Mark asks if I want to babysit a friend's baby. Mike and his wife, Lilly, live near the campus. Mark says it's okay with them if he keeps me company there, and at the same time, I can earn some extra money, which he knows I'll need for next quarter's books. Of course, I say yes, I'll take the job.

The first time we babysit little Diana Myerson, she fell asleep before we came, so her parents put her to bed, and I'm worried that if she wakes up, she'll be terrified. But Lilly, her mom, tells us that the baby always sleeps right through the night. I guess that's how she plans to avoid any fuss before they leave.

Mark and I watch television on their gray, shabby, and lumpy (probably second-hand) sofa, but soon end up more comfortable lying down together on the living room floor covered with wall-to-wall carpeting.

During *The Ed Sullivan Show*, Mark reaches under my blouse and gently holds my right breast in his hand. I don't move or speak until he touches my other breast. "They're both the same," I murmur, and hear him laughing along with the invading voices of the cigarette commercial singing, "Lucky Strike means fine tobacco."

Pretending to fall asleep, I let Mark touch me as he wishes. I'm not frightened, but it feels strange and brings back the scene of Molly and me as little girls in the bathtub together. *"Don't touch there, Carol. Mommy told me no."* Whatever our mother told Molly not to do became an important lesson for me on how to keep myself out of trouble.

What a surprise to discover the pleasurable secrets of my own body with Mark.

"You have magic fingers," I tell him.

"Yes. Now it's your turn."

Suddenly, some overwhelming power is having its way with us. I name it love and welcome it in.

When Mark leaves me at my dorm and goes on across the Midway to his, I feel a deep sense of loss, as if he's now become a part of my being, and the prayerful words "as close as breathing" are more meaningful than ever.

Soon I find it impossible to study without him nearby, and then, when he sings "Black Is the Color of My True Love's Hair" and asks me to "run away" and marry him, it seems ordained.

We decide to elope during the first weekend of Spring Break. We take a train to Buffalo, where I have a cousin who puts us in touch with a rabbi there who tells us if we get a license at City Hall, he'll marry us in his study on Tuesday of that week.

We know our parents will disapprove of our getting married before we graduate, so we decide to go ahead anyway and explain later. Mark is almost certain that his parents will continue to support him through his college career as planned, and with his scholarship and our part-time jobs, he thinks we'll be able to survive and graduate together.

Getting married and being together for one night in a fancy hotel was wonderfully simple; the hard part waited for our return to campus to sort everything out. I can still hear Mark on the phone in the dorm lobby after announcing our marriage to his dad.

"Yes, she's Jewish." (Pause.) "What do you mean 'at least'? Wait a minute. How old were you and Mom? Yeah, well, it was getting rough, Dad. You know what I mean. We love each other. How long could I wait to be with her?" (A longer pause.) "Two years? No way, Dad. Well maybe in your day, okay?"

Mark's voice is now shaking with emotion. "Just tell me, Dad, are you going to bless our marriage and help us or not?" (A very long pause.) I take hold of Mark's arm and pray.

"Okay, well, thank you for your understanding. Tell Mom thanks, too. Yes, of course we will. Why wouldn't we appreciate it? No, her parents can't help us." (Short pause.) "Yes, I'm sure." (Deep breath.) "Goodbye."

Mark looks exhausted but forces a smile. We hug, and then he lifts me up in his arms, saying, "Yes! They're going to help us until we graduate!" A few of our fellow students, sitting close enough to overhear, applaud and take us to Jack's to celebrate.

When I tell Bethie I've become Mrs. Mark Simon, she says

that as far as she's concerned, marriage is a boring form of female servitude, but if that makes me happy, then she wishes me well. She is sitting opposite me in the Goodwill rocking chair in her off-campus apartment, and on the coffee table between us, I notice a package of dog biscuits. For Tarik's dog, I suppose, so she must be still seeing Tarik.

"Don't be afraid to be happy," Bethie advises. "Marriage has a way of doing that to people."

How does Bethie know I find it difficult to believe I deserve to find pleasure in my life, that I worry constantly about potential mishaps joining my real ones?

"Carol, you let problems keep you company. Don't serve them milk and cookies," she jokes, and then advises, "Feed on at least one extreme joy daily. It'll make life seem almost worthwhile."

Is Bethie trying to explain her outrageous pleasure pursuits? I'm wondering now if her magnificent mind needs them daily as the masks to cloak her pain described in her poem.

Certainly, she's right about me. The thought of happiness scares me, a hollow, golden glow coming off it--like in the movies when the young girl from a poor family finally finds her true love or becomes a famous singer just in time to make her family proud, but Technicolor endings seem in stark contrast to the world I know.

Happiness reminds me of the cups in our cabinet that my grandmother gave us the weeks before she died. She would close her eyes, smile, and talk about Russia, where she'd been so happy serving her friends tea in her china cups, pouring from a lovely samovar. When the Cossacks came and her family had to flee, she said they were able to save a few of the cups to remind her of her happy life in Russia. Grandma was always smiling whenever she spoke of the lovely cups she was leaving us, but then she'd end with the warning, "Be very careful when you use them." I never wanted us to use them, afraid they might break and shatter what little happiness they were meant to bring.

Strange how small things like my grandmother's china cups can trigger memories. Whenever I see clothes drying on lines, I'm reminded of Grandma's laundry strung across her kitchen during winters in Utica. We lived in an apartment connected to hers before we moved to Arizona. And thoughts of Grandma's laundry lead on to that one particular day when Grandma's sheets and dresses suddenly grew in stature by becoming my refuge. It happened when Molly's asthma attack interrupted Mom's Mahjong party:

I arrive home from school and open the front door to the wonderful, familiar smell of the cinnamon loaf Mom baked for her friends. Then, just when I'm about to receive a piece of it, Mom hears Molly crying and runs upstairs to help her use "the puffer" to catch her breath.

Soon Mom comes back down with a worried look.

"Carol, come here." She walks me to the bedroom near the parlor to talk, I think so her friends won't hear. "Molly needs the medicine that Dr. Aron ordered for her at Greenfield's Drugstore. You know where. Around the corner by your school. Put back on your boots and your snowsuit and go for it. Max will put it on the charge." Glancing at the cake on the kitchen counter, I hurry by to find my boots. Mom sees and says, "When you come back, we'll cut it."

I dress quickly, excited about going to the drugstore by myself for the first time, and run out, heading for the drugstore with proud thoughts. Mom trusts me. I'm a big girl now like Molly.

It has stopped snowing. I'm on my way and enjoying my slides along the icy stretches on the streets that lead to Greenfield's Drugstore. It's my favorite place because it has stacks of comic books and Max, the pharmacist, gives bubblegum when kids come in with their parents.

When I get to the front of the line, Max smiles at me and says, "Such a pretty little delivery girl." He hands me the bottle of medicine wrapped in a paper bag and gives me a piece of bubblegum.

Hurrying along the slippery streets toward home, I clutch the bag with medicine in my mittened hand, and between slides, I bend to scoop up snow with my other hand. I press it against my legging to form a snowball while blowing bubbles, and I hum parts of our new second-grade song about the Muffin Man who lives in Drury Lane.

When I come to a big mound of glazed-over snow piled high from the big storm a few days before, I climb up on it while remembering when it snowed so high that we couldn't go to school one day. I got to stay home and cut out paper dolls, and even though Molly looked a little pink from her fever, Mom let her out of bed for a little while. Molly had even let me pick out what the Judy Garland doll would wear to the park.

Still thinking about that happy morning, I slide down the glistening, slippery hill, then lose my balance and fall. The bag with the medicine flies out of my hand and lands against an edge of bare sidewalk. When I reach to grab it up, I see the bag and Molly's medicine turn into a purple puddle with sharp edges. I grab a piece and it sticks to my mitten. While I'm shaking it off, it pricks me, and I feel blood dripping into my hand as I run the last block home with my tears streaming down my cheeks. *How can I tell Mom what happened?* She'll be so angry that she won't care about my cut hand, just that I've lost all of Molly's medicine.

While I'm climbing our front steps, I can hear Mom and her friends laughing and clicking Mahjong tiles. Trying to be brave, I wipe my wet face with my mittens. The wool sticks to my cheeks and stings. I open the door and immediately cry out, "Mom, I dropped Molly's medicine."

Mom's face changes into her scariest frown and she groans, "What?"

I run past her and three other faces, and make my way through the house to the back apartment and my grandmother's kitchen, where I can stand between two lines of her wet laundry, hoping it will hide me until Grandma comes home from her shopping.

Mom's Mahjong game is now instantly over. I can hear the goodbyes as her friends leave and then her upset voice phoning Max at the drugstore. Still standing between the rows of Grandma's clothes, I overhear her telling him what I've done. Then I hear her tell him that she'll be there to pick up another bottle of medicine as soon as Grandma comes home.

After Mom puts down the phone, she pokes her head into Grandma's kitchen. She knows I've often taken refuge there, but she doesn't seem to know exactly where I'm hidden. *Will she see my boots and come after me?* I'm standing as still as I can while trembling in fear.

Still at the door, I can see her angry eyes searching for me. Then, she starts to leave, but first she calls out, "Carol, I don't have money for more medicine. If Molly dies, it'll be your fault."

Later, when Grandma comes home, Mom tells her what happened, speaking in her angriest Yiddish, which I clearly understand but never speak. Then, in English she adds, "Max said he'll give me more, no charge."

"God bless him," Grandma says. "And next time go yourself for medicine instead of playing games."

When I hear the front door slam, I come out and run into my grandmother's loving arms.

"Klug nisht, klayna (Don't cry, little one)," she tells me in her sweet Yiddish voice while I sit on her lap, catching my breath between sobs. She helps me out of my boots and snowsuit, and bandages my hand. Then, "Come, Carol," she motions. "We'll go upstairs and see Molly." I don't follow her. I never want to leave Grandma's refuge again. I wait on her bed.

Soon I hear Mom return and tell Grandma, "Max refilled the medicine, no charge." Then she calls out to me, "Carol, I saved you a nice piece of my cinnamon loaf." I figure she isn't angry with me anymore, so I go to where a moment of happiness floats into me like a dream.

* * *

When I phone my parents to tell them that Mark and I were married, I feel my happiness floating away again for a while, just as I expect.

"We would have made you a nice wedding," Mom says.

"We didn't want to wait, Mom. We did have a rabbi do the ceremony, though."

"Okay, I'll tell your dad. But why the hurry? Are you pregnant? I hope not *that*."

"No, Mom." *Not that, but what if?*

Later, my father calls back and wishes us "a long life together of blessings." In his voice I hear the bittersweet mixture of joy and regret. I know he'd hoped for a traditional wedding for me, like Molly's.

THIRTEEN

Not quite a year after Mark and I eloped, I become a mother and Bethie becomes the first Chicago graduate to have earned a bachelor's degree in two years. When she comes to our tiny fourth-floor apartment on Ellis Avenue for a celebration dinner, she exclaims proudly, "I'm free at last to start experiencing real life out there in the jungle." Her first "experiencing" is to begin on a communal farm in Israel. Before she leaves, she calls us from the airport. "In one hour I'll be on my way to Israel to begin my new life speaking a new language in a new land. Shalom Chicago!"

"Shalom Bethie!" I say, caught up in her excitement.

She promises she will write, and soon her letters begin arriving from a kibbutz, which she explains is a collective farm community she has joined in Israel. Soon she is writing about plucking chickens and cleaning bathrooms, and how much she hates her work on the kibbutz but is fascinated with her new Israeli friends.

"They are wonderful to me," she writes, and later, "They can't believe how quickly I've learned to speak Hebrew. It's nothing like the antique Hebrew you read in your prayer book, except the alphabet, of course, and many root words."

I read her letters without envy. Mark and my baby daughter

Wendy have become my world while I continue my university studies part-time.

A few months later, Bethie's letters change. She stops writing about new adventures and begins relating situations she then finds absurd or frustrating.

"My friend Galeet worries about her children all the time. There is no reason for it as they are well cared for in the kibbutz nursery. Galeet says to worry is a normal expression of a mother's love, but I'm guessing it's guilt. Still, there's a lot of kids crying for their parents at night, my friends working in the nursery say."

In the very next letter, "Miriam hates me now because I slept with her boyfriend." It was *his* idea, Carol. I told her he was like that, but she didn't believe me. I did her a favor really by showing her. Does that make me a whore? I guess in Biblical times, they would stone girls like me. Horrible, to think that, but they do it even now in some Arab countries."

Then Bethie mentions the possibility of her having to leave the kibbutz. I guess that's how it's solved nowadays. However, she adds that the kibbutz voted to send her to Hebrew University to work on her thesis. "It would mean a short bus ride two days a week and making up the time doing my chores. I would really welcome doing it, but I feel I'll owe the kibbutz something in return. What?"

In her next letter, she complains about a new rocking chair she purchased and is required to put in the kibbutz lounge. "I paid plenty of shekels for it and had it shipped from Tel Aviv. Now it's available to a hundred other people. Obviously a foolish move on my part. I don't think I like all this sharing."

Just when I think she'll probably be coming home soon, her

letters sound happier. She is now a student at Hebrew University, where she's met Reuben Kalig, a fellow student who had been helped to escape from Stalin's Russia. Bethie writes, "His mother left him, only a few days old, in a basket on the front steps of an orphanage right after the war. She never returned for him. No one knew who she was, or his father. Who cares anyway, I say. Reuben is very handsome and clever, and we have a lot in common. For one thing, we both hate our mothers. Now don't think I'm giving in to stupid conventions. I'm just marrying Reuben so he can come to the US. But I'm keeping my own last name and if we decide to stay together, we don't plan to have any children."

When her letters stop coming, I assume that Bethie and Reuben got married and will be in the States after she graduates. Knowing Bethie, I also assume that won't take long, and they'll appear on campus together or at our apartment, and we'll meet Reuben.

I assumed wrong. Occasionally, over the next four years, holiday cards come to us from Bethie and Reuben from various places in Europe. I answer them with our cards, putting a letter in each one, but Bethie never responds to any of my letters.

During that time, I'm very busy having two more babies and taking some journalism classes at night even though it doesn't seem as if I will ever have enough time for a newspaper job again, and my dancing, choreography, and poetry just fade into the past like outgrown toys.

Now I'm shopping at the grocery store almost daily since Mark has returned from a company-paid engineering conference in France insisting that I buy only the very freshest French bread, and since the children balk at vegetables, I search for the crispiest lettuce. Grocery shelves, lines, and cash registers haunt my dreams.

I go to appointments with doctors and teachers, and these once-normal kinds of problems don't feel normal anymore.

Mark can't seem to break into screenwriting. Having a full-time regular job makes it harder, but I continue giving him feedback on his scripts and encouraging him not to give up. "Just find another agent," I suggest each time the rejection letters cloud his day.

* * *

One holiday weekend, Bethie calls from Los Angeles and soon appears at our house in Irvine, where Mark has recently landed a higher paying aerospace job with a major firm in the area. In my last greeting card to Bethie, I'd given her our new address.

Whenever I play back her visit, I'm filled with regrets.

Light streams in on her sharpened features framed in chunks of golden hair. The chopped look. She is very trim, dressed in a black suit, dark stockings, and shoes with wedge heels. I never saw her look so stylish and professional. We hug.

"Bethie, you look great!"

She hardly glances at me, and I'm glad because I'm still in my jeans and an old maternity top after doing yard work. I'm not trim or even marginally in fashion.

"Where's Reuben?" I ask, looking down the empty walkway. "Isn't he here with you?"

""No," she says sharply. Then, as we walk into the kitchen, she explains, "That's over, Carol, except for the legal side of it, and what a drag that's been."

We sit down over coffee and try to recapture our easy conversation. We both seem to see immediately that it's impossible but continue trying.

"So, it's motherhood for you, station wagon and all."

"Yes," I say proudly. "My children keep me busy."

"You like that?"

"Mostly...but sometimes it's hard."

"Hard? I would think boring."

"Aren't all jobs boring at times? Mark gets tired of his job, too."

"Are you still writing?" she asks.

"Not much. I can't seem to get going again."

Her eyes focus on mine. Her tone, more serious now, has a sharper edge to it than I remember. I'm thinking this must be because we were younger then and she has traveled, married, become a professor, is divorced. And, I guess to her I'm someone else too now.

"You're a born poet, Carol. You've got to write."

I don't answer her, but it hurts to realize that she's clearly disappointed in who I've become.

"Well, what about your dancing? Weren't you once involved in some choreography work?"

Pleased she remembers, I reply, "That seems like a thousand years ago, Bethie. My job now is to raise my kids so they'll have a chance to do what they want with their lives."

I start telling her about my children, but soon it's clear she is only politely interested, so I change the subject and ask, "What about your marriage to Reuben? Why didn't it work out?"

"He's inept," she says, her mouth twisting to the side as she bites at her bottom lip, seeming to avoid further expressions of anger by not saying more, and I want to comfort her, but I don't know what to say.

During this awkward silence, Wendy appears at the door, and I am relieved and proudly introduce her.

"She's fabulous," Bethie says with her arms extended to hug Wendy, surprising me with her sudden enthusiasm.

"I am," Wendy agrees, laughing but pushing away and throwing back her head, which tosses her long, honey-brown pigtails in the air. Then she runs to me and climbs into my lap, and soon she's involved in her usual habit of adding sugar and cream to my coffee and drinking most of it while she chatters about her day at school.

Bethie listens looking enchanted. "You're really wonderful," she tells Wendy after hearing the amusing way Wendy relates her school adventures.

Next, Wendy invites Bethie to inspect her new Star of David pendant and then her notebook.

"All A's?"

From then on, they are friends.

I look on, smiling and amazed at how similarly their minds seem to work and how much they enjoy each other.

Bethie tells us at dinner that she hopes to stay with us for a week, then fly back to New York to visit another friend. When Mark brings up the subject of Reuben, she says, "He's inept. He couldn't even hold a job. I got tired of supporting him." She hesitates, then decides to add, "He'll probably sue me for alimony." Mark and I are wide-eyed with astonishment. "Can he do that?" he asks.

"Yes," she nods, "because I've been supporting him."

"On what?

"On my salary."

"What do you do?" He sounds too surprised.

Bethie, looking annoyed at Mark, tells him, "I'm a professor of linguistics at the University of New Mexico, and I've published some research and also a textbook."

"I never got a card from New Mexico," I say, hoping to change the tone of the conversation. "How come?"

Bethie shrugs. "Too busy with the divorce. And with my little vacation trips down to Mexico. I have to have some fun, you know." We all laugh in agreement.

"Have you two been to Mexico? It's great!"

"I hear it's a great place to get laid," Mark says.

I look with raised eyebrows at him, then notice Bethie's smile, and her nod in acknowledgement. I'm glad Wendy has finished her dinner and left to do homework.

"Mm, this beef stew is delicious," Bethie says. "I really love food cooked like this."

"She's a wonderful cook and a wonderful mother," Mark chimes with compliments.

"Well thanks, both of you," I say, a little embarrassed, "but the cake I baked for dessert didn't quite measure up to my mom's great recipe. It didn't rise like it should and I can't figure out why."

"I'm sure it'll be fine," Bethie reassures. "Your mother's

marble cake?" When I nod, she says, "I remember it so well. It can't be bad, Carol. Bring it on."

After dinner, Bethie asks Mark if he knows anyone she can go out with while in California. He says yes, that he has someone in mind, a colleague who'd asked him once about one of the secretaries in his bay. "I'd suggested Peggy, my secretary, but, I guess nothing came of it since now she's dating someone else. I don't think Arnold's going steady with anyone."

Later that evening, with everyone sleeping except Bethie and me, we sit out on the back porch with what's left of a bottle of wine from dinner, and she tells me Reuben's story: He'd been abandoned as a newborn at a Soviet orphanage in 1944 along with a flood of other babies whose parents had been sent to Siberia or killed.

Until Reuben was fourteen years old, he received a minimum of food, clothing, and schooling, along with a heavy dose of military preparedness training. Shortly before his fifteenth birthday, a Jewish couple, who were sent from some Israeli rescue organization, came to the orphanage asking to foster some Jewish children. They had plans to take them to Israel and had brought cash to encourage a quick departure, but only one boy, Reuben, had been allowed to leave with them. Reuben thought it was because he'd been circumcised, which proved he'd been a Jewish baby.

In less than a year Reuben would have been taken into the Russian army if one of the caregivers, who he said loved him, hadn't been bribed to help him go.

When he got to Israel, he stayed with the couple, who taught him to speak Hebrew and English, and it wasn't long before they helped get him a part-time job tutoring in Russian language studies at Hebrew University, where he met Bethie.

"The beginning of the end," Bethie says. "I married him to bring him here. And then, a year later, it was all over. He even borrowed money from my dad and never paid him back. What a loser."

"I'm sorry."

"My choice. I'm not sorry," she says, lifting her chin, and her response echoes of when she first spoke about Alex's death. *I'm not sorry.*

"In your letters, you seemed to care about Reuben."

"Cared enough to marry him and bring him here, but I didn't realize he was a damaged kid, raised without a mother, only a caretaker. I tried to help him, but he couldn't handle it, lost job after job, making the same stupid mistakes again and again. *Once* is a learning thing, Carol, but *twice* is dumb, and after that, it's a sickness. He just didn't want to work. When I complained, he said I was all the work he needed. And, on top of all that, he wasn't much of a lover either. He would…"

"Well then, I guess that was it!" I say, hoping to stop her from telling me more bedroom stuff.

* * *

Today, Mark invited Arnold for dinner to meet Bethie, and he comes to the door with a nice bottle of white wine and a bouquet of pink roses. "For you," he says, handing them to me. "Thanks for having me." He has a strong, smooth manner and is fairly trim, but not at all handsome. In fact, his eyes seem too small for his broad face and his teeth too large for his mouth. He smiles as I welcome him in, and he follows me to the kitchen to find a vase for the flowers and put the wine in the refrigerator to chill.

Mark soon joins us and offers him a drink before dinner, and they return to the living room with their glasses and a bowl of nuts while I go upstairs to tuck Daniel into bed and check on little Judd.

Wendy has been given the honor of staying up for a late dinner. "I want to meet Daddy's guest from work with Bethie," she announces, putting on her party dress and shoes while I wait to comb her hair with ribbons. When Bethie comes into the bedroom, Wendy exclaims, "Oh, you look so pretty!" Then, "Mom, can I wear earrings too?"

Bethie has on a slim black sleeveless dress with a white pearl necklace, dangling earrings and shiny, black high-heeled pumps. She looks like a gorgeous model in a fashion magazine, like someone I don't know.

"Nice," I say to her, managing to hide my jealous amazement. Then, "No on the earrings, Wendy. Not until you're older."

"How does Arnold look?" Bethie asks.

"Let's go down and you'll see," I tell her.

I think Arnold is more surprised when he sees Bethie than I was. He doesn't take his eyes off her until I serve my baked apple tart for dessert.

"A great dinner, Carol," Arnold says. "I seldom have a home-cooked meal. What a treat!" He then asks Bethie if she'd like to go with him to see an art film playing somewhere in Costa Mesa. From the start, she'd acted cool toward him, but she accepts his invitation. They decide to leave immediately after dessert in order to make the show on time, and Bethie asks for a key, saying, "So I don't wake anybody when I come in."

I wake up when the sprinklers go on. Soon I hear Bethie come up the stairs to Wendy's room to occupy the empty twin bed we planned for her stay. Glancing at the clock near my bed, I see the time. It's 4:00 a.m.

At noon, when Bethie comes downstairs to have some breakfast, she soon informs me that she hopes to see Arnold again before she goes back to Albuquerque.

"I guess you like him then, huh?"

She doesn't answer, just smiles and takes another bite of toast.

Afterwards, while I'm nursing baby Judd, she comes to sit with us on the sofa. At first she seems edgy, and I think maybe the nursing is making her uncomfortable, but I soon learn that isn't the cause when she coyly asks me if she might borrow my car overnight and explains, "I want to meet Arnold somewhere, instead of having him pick me up here."

Curious about that, but not wanting to press her, I wait for her to tell me more. I'm not her mother, I tell myself, but still, the tone of her request leads me to wonder what it's going to be like having her stay here with us for the rest of the week and doing her private things while using my car. *Could she be into drugs? If so, at least she doesn't want to do them here. What if Wendy saw? Best to give her the keys.*

"Yes," I say after an awkward moment of silence. "You can borrow my car since I won't need it until...maybe not until tomorrow afternoon." I wait again to be given more information, hopefully less scary, but she just thanks me and goes upstairs to get dressed.

When Bethie comes back downstairs, Daniel is in the bathtub shouting, "Mom, you said you'd bring my motorboats!" Bethie's all dressed up again, this time wearing black suede, heeled boots and a long black skirt, a white silk blouse and a black knitted stole.

"You look wonderful!" I say when I hand her my keys. She thanks me for the compliment and leaves.

Daniel, having lost hope in my delivery of his bathtub boats by this time, is standing outside the tub completely covered with soapsuds and with a large puddle of water covering and surrounding his feet. I guide him back into the tub and hand him the boats. Together, we wind them all up at once, and while the red and blue boats gurgle and race around him, he laughs.

When I manage to lure him out of the tub with a promise of his favorite flavor of ice cream, I wrap him in a big towel and hug him close.

Feeling strangely upset, but comforted by his loving arms around my neck, I carry him to his room and sit with him there until he grows restless and slides off my lap to find his pajamas.

Still unsettled, I review my conversation with Bethie that troubled me so much. Can I be that jealous? But why? I have Mark and our three children. Still, I see Bethie's free lifestyle in glaring contrast to the many responsibilities I have as a wife and mother. But what has happened to the rest of me, the

Carol that Bethie knew and expected to see? Have I lost a part of myself? And if yes, it's true that I have, I wonder if she's worth trying to find again.

Interrupting my thoughts, Wendy appears with a letter in hand. "From Grandma. She's bringing me a new dress when she comes for Passover. I'm going to look beautiful in it, Grandma says." Another jealous twinge, but I quickly defeat it with Bethie's warning, *Don't let her mess with you.* And I won't let her mess with Wendy and me, either!

I tell Wendy, "Grandma's right about that. Whatever you're wearing, you'll always look as beautiful to me as the day you were born and I first held you in my arms."

At noon the following day, Bethie returns with my car. We lunch together over tuna sandwiches and a bottle of Chablis, which is helping us to talk more easily, so I say again, "I guess you must like Arnold."

"Not much," she says, "but he's okay for a visit."

"But you were out with him *all* last night!"

"So what?" she laughs. "He's okay. Better than nothing, right? I'm not going to become a divorced nun. Nobody should expect me to give up sex for any reason. I believe we women need it as much as men do." Then, before biting into her sandwich again, she adds, "Really, Carol. Arnold's okay…for now."

"I would worry about doing something like that."

"Like what? Casual sex? It's the best, Carol. But I guess you wouldn't know about that, would you?"

"Casual? Isn't that an oxymoron? Sex isn't casual. It creates life, can destroy families, spread diseases, even cause death."

"I know how to take care of myself," she murmurs, then suddenly turns pale and continues in a tone so unlike herself. "I don't ever want children, and since I'm not religious," she reminds. "I don't worry about divine retribution. She takes a sip of her coffee and her color and confidence return. "All that emotional stuff, Carol, will soon be outdated. Sex will be advertised on TV, accepted by all but the most backwardly religious."

I shrug and get up to make some fresh coffee.

"I guess you're still pretty religious though," she says. "I noticed that Wendy wears a star."

"She loves it. My father gave it to her."

"Yeah, well, she'll probably wear it to some goddamn job interview someday and get messed over because of it."

"What do you mean?" It's painful to hear her talk that way about anything to do with Wendy.

"I mean she'll be labeled a 'Jewish Princess.' Have you ever heard the demeaning way people talk about them?"

"Only ignorant people!"

With my stomach churning, I start to turn away, but she touches my arm. "Listen, even Jewish comedians think they have some sanctified right to ridicule Jewish women. Trust me, Carol, it'll backfire by the time Wendy grows up. You'll see. All those repulsive jokes will become stereotypes of girls like Wendy, filling her with self-hatred. You'll have to be Carol again to help her deal with it, not a mother lost in a sink of dishes."

Stunned by her words, I just stare at her until she begins to laugh. *At me, I think. She's laughing at me. If I try to answer her, I'll reveal my uncertainty until without even trying, she'll destroy whatever is holding me together now.*

I want her to leave.

While clearing the table of our lunch dishes, I attack. "So, where are you off to on Monday, Bethie? What grand adventure is Professor Hartung off to experience?"

A look of realization spreads across her face. I see the hurt in her eyes and immediately regret what I did.

"I have a friend from UofC whom I've kept in touch with, Greta Shulburg. She lives in Rochester now. I'll call Greta and invite her to spend some time with me tomorrow in New York. I'll get us tickets to some plays."

"Sounds great," I say, pouring coffee into our cups. She drinks hers hurriedly and goes upstairs.

The next morning, Bethie phones her friend Greta, then, over my objections, gives me ten dollars to cover the call, and insists, again over my objections, that she'll take a cab to the airport.

When the cab comes and we say our cool goodbyes, I watch Bethie climb into the back seat to be driven away. It hurts to see her move out of sight, but it hurt more having her with us, knowing how disappointed she is in the choices I've made for myself and for Wendy.

After a while, more regrets spread over me as I play back that last painful scene a thousand times. I'm asking myself why I didn't break through that awful silence, tell her how I felt and not let her leave until we were able to talk about what happened between us.

Now, the only way I'm able to handle what happened is to

remind myself that our friendship is too important to both of us for it to suddenly end over this one upsetting conversation. I assume that one of us will eventually call or write to apologize and everything between us will soon again be okay.

I assumed wrong.

I would never see Bethie again.

FOURTEEN

After another silent ordeal with Dr. Kelly, I'm wondering where to begin talking about my friendship with Bethie and her strange marriage to Reuben when he asks, "Wouldn't you like to try some group therapy? Even if you don't want to talk, you may even be helped by just listening. Some of my patients don't share at the first few sessions, but say later they found it helpful to hear what others in the group were sharing."

I ask for more specifics, and he suggests, "Well, your friend Jenna's group plans to go to San Diego next weekend. The university there is offering a training weekend for professionals and others interested in the group therapy method formulated by Carl Rogers."

"I don't trust groups."

"Yes, but I think that being with Jenna may help you feel more secure. Why not give it a try? You don't even have to say anything if you're uncomfortable."

When I mention Kelly's idea to Mark, he thinks I should do it, and Jenna reminds me, "Time without kids, Carol. We'll really have time to talk on the way. Please say yes."

After hearing Mark and Jenna's further urging, I'm thinking I should go as a listener. It's an opportunity to be there with Jenna. We'll be rooming together and going out for our meals together, talking afterwards about our reactions to the sessions. It might actually be kind of fun.

During the drive to San Diego, Jenna rehearses me for what she calls therapy lingo.

"It's important not to generalize," she explains. "Say 'I,' never say 'We.'"

"Or what?" I begin to panic. Carson McCullers, one of my favorite novelists, refers to the "we of me" in her book *A Member of the Wedding*. That's how Frankie, the young girl in the story, says she relates to people she doesn't know...through a universal human bond. I find that idea very insightful. Am I now going to be asked to eradicate that kind of inspiration from my life?

"Someone will probably call you on it, that's all."

"What about 'We the people'? Is that outdated?"

"That's the point, Carol," Jenna explains. "No speeches. Just a sharing from one's personal perspective is all that's required in a group of this kind."

"Maybe." I doubt that I will remember not to generalize about anything all weekend, but Jenna there to nudge me offers some hope.

"Oh, one more rule," Jenna says. "When you want to give your opinion, don't begin with 'I think that...so on and so forth.' Instead say, 'I am fantasizing that...'"

"Why? It sounds crazy, or even sexual."

"Only at first. Soon you'll get used to it. I suppose seeing it as possibly just a fleeting idea is less intimidating to some in the group."

Jenna drives on to the next little town, where we decide to stop for coffee. "We'll get there too early if we go straight on," she figures. "Our room won't be ready. We might as well enjoy the trip."

"I'm too anxious to enjoy this, Jenna."

While we have coffee, Jenna decides to have lunch. "No point," she decides, "in wandering around looking for the cafeteria when we have loads of time to have lunch here."

I'm too nervous to eat lunch anywhere, but I order a coffee and muffin to keep her company.

"Do you really like doing that kind of thing?" I ask while I watch her gather her tuna salad into a folded slice of bread, count out nine potato chips from the bag she bought to go along with her salad, and place them on her plate. It's obvious that Jenna has changed her diet again. Last time we had lunch together, she was on grapefruit and hard-boiled eggs. Always dieting, she never seems to lose any weight.

Jenna, a former medical receptionist, is married to a pilot. Now he flies all over the world (resting here and there with young stewardesses, Jenna thinks) while she stays home to carry out their plan to raise a family and give her the opportunity to draw her wonderful charcoal sketches. She once had gleefully admitted to me that when she found out about John's affairs from one of her friends, she began drawing hideous sketches that resembled him, and soon after that, she decided to see Dr. Kelly. With five years of therapy, she's moved on, she's proud to say, to doing sketches of other men. I've seen them and they're quite good.

"John's upset about my nude models," she shares with a smile. "I guess I've finally got his attention."

As we drive through the tiny beach cities before Carlsbad, I ask, "Do you like group therapy?"

"I wouldn't say 'group' is fun," she replies, "but I look forward to my session each week, and Dr. Kelly is a unique kind of facilitator. He makes sure everyone in the group feels comfortable when talking about their pain. And who wants to lay all that stuff on regular friends? But it feels okay to be sharing it in the group. In fact, I'm planning to work on something this weekend."

"Work?" A warning of some kind?

"Yes, on my problems. Sometimes I don't have the energy. But maybe this weekend."

I'm guessing now that the weekend won't be as simple as it sounded when Dr. Kelly advised me to go, saying, "Give yourself a chance to feel more comfortable in a group." Will Jenna feel comfortable sharing her pain with me there? And how will I feel about hearing?

We arrive just in time for the orientation speeches.

The first unexpected tremor comes when Jenna and I are separated to ensure, we're told, a kind of random grouping that might be a better test for the counselors in training. We count off by the suggested number system. Since Jenna is standing behind me in line, she goes with one group and I go with another. So much for her help. I'm now suddenly feeling very vulnerable as twenty of us parade down a long hallway and into a classroom.

Immediately, some in my group rearrange the chairs from traditional rows to a doubled, semi-circular pattern. They seem to know what's required. Some kind of Rogerian prescription, I figure, standing near the door and watching. Part of the work Jenna talked about, I want to think, but really know it isn't.

When seated in our half-circles, I glance around, studying the other members of my assigned group. The majority are women who look to be in their early thirties, but there are three men, all younger. Dressed like students, they are wearing jeans, bulky sweaters, and tennis shoes. One woman wearing a pleated skirt and boots with flat heels seems already acquainted with the young man sitting near her. She is turning to him and whispering something. Lucky her to know someone, I'm thinking. Did one of them change places in line? Smart.

Soon the room becomes absolutely quiet.

I've never been with so many people who remain silent for so long. I wait, scanning the faces for signs of what might happen next. Nothing happens. No one speaks up. The group sits almost motionless for at least another five minutes.

Finally, unable to stand it any longer, I turn to the young man in front of me holding a clipboard and ask, "Are you our designated leader?"

"No," he replies sharply, "I'm just a facilitator. Why do you ask?"

Everyone listens as I, who have come only to listen and observe, feel forced to respond to what sounds to me like a challenge.

"Well, aren't we ever going to begin?"

"Why don't *you* begin? Introduce yourself."

"I'm Carol Mandell." My knees are shaking as I wait for some response from anyone. None. A long silence again. Then he who had called himself a facilitator asks sharply if I want to tell "us" why I came.

At this point, I have to speak or surrender to what promises to continue as a painfully mute situation.

"I came because I want to feel more at ease talking with people in a group setting," I say. "This is very hard for me. This...this is very hard for me." I search the faces around me for signs of warmth. The woman next to me now has moved her chin down near her folded arms. The man on her right has turned to look out the window. Those two are enough for me to decide to give up and stop talking.

Again, we're all sitting in silence.

Suddenly, as if coming out of a trance, a red-haired, slim woman calls out, "I'm ready to work."

Our facilitator invites her to come up to the front of the room. Two chairs are set up and she sits in one of them and faces the other one without saying anything until the woman next to me looks up and asks, "Who do you want to dialogue with, Rose?"

That's when I realize that most of the others in the room are acquainted and that most of them have been to these Rogerian sessions many times before. I can tell by their comfort with the lingo and how they know each other's names that some may even be practicing therapists who have come for a refresher weekend or to "work" on their own problems.

"I want to dialogue with my baby," Rose tells us. She confides that she'd decided on an abortion in the early weeks of her pregnancy. "It was a long time ago, but it still hurts," she cries while telling us.

She begins speaking to her lost fetus in the empty chair and soon becomes hysterical, crying, "I killed you, my baby, with that abortion."

Immediately, tissues are offered. She takes one and blows her nose, then continues crying, "I hated your father for deserting me," then confesses to her fetal ghost, "You were so tiny, only six weeks old and I had you destroyed." And now she is weeping uncontrollably and falling from her chair to the floor.

This all happens so fast that it takes me a few minutes to overcome my shock and jump up from my seat to try to comfort her. I'm stopped by our so-called facilitator, who calls out, "Carol, you need to sit back down."

"Then *you* do something," I beg. "Please, help her."

"Rose needs to continue her work on this now," he announces. Then, turning to me, he says, "Please sit down and allow her to do that."

I sit back down.

After another short silence, Rose's sobbing begins again. I can't make myself sit there and just listen. I call out to the facilitator, "Do something, please!"

This time he stands and holds his hand up in front of my face as if to stop me from going on and calls over his shoulder, "Sorry, Rose." Then, "Everyone, let's break for an hour. We'll resume at two o'clock."

I stand in front of my chair feeling foolish while everyone files out, even Rose, who has taken the offered hand of one woman as they leave.

With the rest of the group gone, the facilitator stops in front of me and shakes his head. "You need to read more about this therapy before you speak."

"Why? Is it a game or something?"

"No, but I think that…"

"You mean you *fantasize* that…"

He shrugs and walks out.

When Jenna opens the door to our assigned dorm room, I'm sitting on the bed and crying. After managing between sobs to explain why I'm upset, I tell her, "I can't stay. I'll take the bus back to Irvine."

Jenna insists on going home with me. "I'm not really working at all," she says, "so I might as well."

When I get home, still very upset, I tell Mark that I won't be going back to see Dr. Kelly.

Later that evening, Mark is concerned enough about me to phone my father, something he never does, and from our bedroom, I hear his anxious voice suggesting, "It might help if you talk to her. Maybe she'll listen to you." A pause. Then, "How soon can you come?"

FIFTEEN

Dad comes the next day.

As soon as he walks in, I see his worried face, handsome as always though his hair has turned mostly gray. He reaches out to hug me. I cling to him until the children come in and circle us with their chatter. Soon he's smiling at them while opening his suitcase and handing them their gifts.

Later, Mark takes the children out for a drive and lunch so that Dad and I are left alone to talk.

Probably seeing I'm not my usual, helpful self, Dad goes about the kitchen preparing a plate of crackers and cheese, and then takes out a couple of bottles of beer for us. "Let's have a little picnic, Carol," he says. You always liked our picnics together. Remember?"

While he carries the tray out to the backyard, safe moments from childhood come to mind--like the times when he would allow me a sip of his beer on Friday afternoons.

He always seemed happy then, the hard work week behind him, a peaceful Sabbath ahead for prayer and study, and Mom's special meal.

After a little food and the beer, I feel better, and I start to want to talk to him about Bethie.

"I feel some place inside me is empty now that Bethie is gone, Dad."

"Yes. Mark told me you're taking the loss of your friend very hard." He takes my hand.

"Dad, she killed herself. Do you remember Bethie? She's dead!" I surprise myself using Dr. Kelly's directness. Maybe he did help me a little with that.

"May she rest in peace," he replies with the traditional response when mentioning a dead loved one's name. "I guess she lost faith, your friend. She didn't believe things would change."

His simplistic view of Bethie's plight angers me. I pull my hand away and stand up. "She never had faith," I tell him. "I'm not sure I do." I know it's hard for him to hear me announcing this, but I'm too upset to care. Seeing his continued calm, I'm encouraged to press on. "How can you be so sure, Dad...about God?"

"I'm not so sure," he admits for the first time. "But what do I have to lose?"

Exactly "Pascal's Wager," I realize. Not bad for a carpenter to conclude on his own. With new respect, I take a deep breath and sit down next to him again.

"My faith gives me hope, Carol," he continues, "but faith and hope have nothing to do with knowing."

"Descartes, the famous French philosopher, would disagree, Dad," I answer. "He said, 'I think, therefore, I am.' In other words, to think is how we know we're alive."

"He was wrong, Carol," he says, now challenging Descartes with confidence, and even in my anxious state of mind, I eagerly await his argument. Am I dreaming, I wonder, sitting in my garden talking seventeenth-century philosophy with my dad?

"According to our faith," he continues, "God told Moses 'I AM THAT I AM.' So how can we be any more than that? In His image, we are that we are. That's why thinking doesn't always help."

Seeing my puzzled look, he gives me some supporting examples. "Think too much about walking, and you'll probably trip. Right?"

I nod and reluctantly smile to hear him add, "Think too much about talking, you might stutter." He concludes his argument with, "Where there's life, there's hope, Carol. Things are always changing. Your friend, may she rest in peace, didn't understand this. She lost hope."

He begins to recite the ancient Hebrew prayer for the dead, and I join in, praying with him for the first time in many years. "Yit gadal ve'yit kadash…." The words have no exact meaning to me, and there are no precise words that speak to the faith of my father in his God. I understand them on some deeper level as voiced rhythms of generations past so intricately synthesized, they can never be undone, even by someone like me, so full of doubt but standing here beside him, his voice enjoining me with the God of a childhood prayer who stays even beyond belief "as close as breathing."

Afterward, feeling a part of my life returning to me, I reach for my father's hand. His prayers for Bethie have become mine, and I want to let her "rest in peace."

When we finish eating, Dad says, "Your mother's arthritis makes it harder now for her to keep up with things in the house. Eventually, we may have to move to a smaller place." He stands and puts our empty glasses and the dish of leftover crackers on the tray. "Please try to understand her a little," he persists, "and forgive her."

I turn away, hoping he won't notice the tears his request has evoked. "I'll try, Dad," I tell him, just to give him the small hope I know will end his plea, but a childhood dream whispers to me again that one day I will suddenly remember or find something--a snapshot of Mom and me sitting in the park together, or remember her holding my face in her hands and saying, "What a fine little girl." Still filled with these half-orphan dreams, I long to cry out to her, "Mother, my must-have-been refuge from despair, I have no pictures of your kisses now, no close-ups of our cheeks. I want to throw away this anger. Why can't I remember?" All my hopes for her love were buried deep in a dark place where I finally put them to sleep, but now I hear her calling again, the word *mother* vibrating in me like a tortured violin.

Bethie once said, "What a sad note you keep playing. Your mother's never going to change. Believe me, I know."

"You can't know that," I replied. Then I remembered the one night I'd slept at her house when she already knew what I still can't seem to learn.

Now Mom and I keep in touch long distance, our words measured in time, in their cost to us, both careful to keep the space we both reserve for me to become a woman. I send her birthday cards each year, thankful to find something appropriately written in a commercial voice, my own voice freed from the words I'd locked away even before my small breasts began to swell.

As if Dad read my thoughts while he carried the loaded snack tray into the house, he repeats, "It's time to forgive, Carol."

"I'm trying, Dad," I manage again to reassure him while looking into his eyes for a small glimmer of hope.

While Dad is staying with us, all three of my children are falling in love with their grandfather, and each is having a special interaction with him.

My dad loves singing songs to little Judd, who sings along in a humming sound that is right on key. We were all amazed when we first heard him, and now it's becoming Judd's signature in the family. For the first time, he has earned a distinctive role, which may one day earn him a place in the Community Opera Chorus. Or maybe he'll be cast in the role of The Holy Fool, who sings as the soul of the Russian people in the opera Boris Godunov. Could all that begin this week?

Also this week, Daniel's soccer team is scheduled to compete in the Junior Soccer League playoffs, but he can't play because he hurt his knee a few days ago during a game. After a crying jag, he's ended up angry at everyone around him and refusing to eat dinner. I can't seem to do the mothering I always did whenever my children were upset, but Dad is stepping in for me, bringing them ice cream and comic books, and while Mark is at work, Dad fills in. He takes Daniel to the doctor and then to the toy store.

When Daniel learns that Dad is leaving at the end of the week, he cries. Dad promises him he can come and stay with him in Tucson during the summer and he'll teach him to ride horses.

Mark and I enjoy seeing how the boys take to my dad, but when we happen to overhear a long conversations with Wendy and him, we're really amazed. She always has so many questions we find difficult to answer, but Dad has no trouble. His spiritual wisdom seems to flow naturally from the center of his being.

When Wendy arrives home from Sunday School and goes immediately to find her grandpa, he's reading his portable Bible under a tree in the backyard, and I'm making lunch in the kitchen. From an open window, I see Wendy run over and sit next to him. I can hear their whole conversation.

"Grandpa, tell me something," Wendy says in her most serious, challenging voice. "How could God have created the whole world and all its creatures in only six days? I don't believe that, do you?" She sounds so much like Bethie, it shakes me to the core.

"Well, Granddaughter," he responds, closing his book and putting his arm around her, "this is something we really need to talk about for a long time, but now, let's you and I get started." Wendy looks very excited, while Dad remains his peaceful self. And I, leaning on the window ledge forget about putting mustard on bologna sandwiches, and listen, fascinated. It's like watching myself in a scene from my childhood.

"Of course, Wendy, we can't know about God with any certainty, but we can have faith that what we believe is true, and that's good if it makes us kind and strong. Like our prophet Micah tells us, all God wants is that we do justly, be kind and merciful, and walk with humility."

"What's humility?"

"The opposite of arrogance."

"What's arrogance?" Wendy laughs while still very involved in Dad's every word.

"Being arrogant is not seeing ourselves as just a small part of all the animals, plants, and peoples of the world in this vast universe."

"Grandpa, what about all that stuff about being created in just six days? How could that happen? Do you believe that?

"Maybe one day to us is like millions and millions of years of creation; it probably took that long for so many different kinds of life to happen. Maybe God, the creator, had to work that all out, make things from other things, test them until they became stronger and survived until..."

"Until he created us? Cause we're the best of all, aren't we?"

"Careful, now, Wendy. Remember about humility?"

"Whoops!"

Their conversation continues over lunch.

Before Wendy runs off to play with her neighbor friend waiting at the door, she tells Dad, "I guess I'll have a lot to explain to everyone next week at Sunday School."

After she leaves, Dad remarks, "You know, Carol, she's a smart little girl, like you were. Always questioning. That's good. Will she have a Bat Mitzvah? Be called to read the Torah?"

"Molly and I didn't."

"Well, Wendy could. I'll teach her to read Hebrew each time I come. She'll learn fast, I can tell."

"You're a good teacher, Dad."

"And I'm a pretty good carpenter, too," he adds. "You'll see, I fixed a lot of things while I was here."

"Mark gave you a long list--too long, really--but we both appreciate everything you've done for us."

"My pleasure."

SIXTEEN

Although my father's visit comforted me, I'm struggling again to come to terms with Bethie's desperate decision. Like the biblical Jacob, I wrestle with an angel each night. Is Bethie's spirit trying to tell me something? I need to know why Bethie wanted to die.

She was so brilliant and so brave about accepting life's challenges. *It's all a game to me... I like it that way.*

Was it
one angry wish
or some unsettled debt
to stamp forever on our heads
regret?

After writing many more cinquains to Bethie and putting them in a little chapbook that Jenna offered to decorate with sketches drawn from pictures of Bethie and flowers around some of the poems, I decide to try contacting Greta Shulburg.

Luckily, she's listed in the Rochester directory.

When Greta hears my name, she immediately knows who I am

and why I'm calling. "You've heard about Bethie, I suppose. She often spoke about her friend Carol living in California."

"Bethie sent me a letter postmarked the day before she died."

"You too? I got a really nasty one," Greta says. "Guilt trip and all." Her voice quivers and she now sounds upset when telling me, "Bethie said I'd let her down by not inviting her to stay with us after her operation."

"What operation?" I ask, revealing how much I had lost touch. *I'll be your friend forever.*

"Her hysterectomy. Didn't she tell you?"

Although shaken now with surprise, I manage to admit we'd argued and lost touch two years before the letter came. Greta says she knew about Bethie's situation during that time. "She had a terrible doctor. He took out everything, Bethie told me, to make sure that she'd be okay. I guess she was very badly infected. Bethie thought the doctors weren't even sure of the exact cause. She'd slept around a lot, went down to Mexico so people at the university wouldn't gossip. She worried about losing her position there. Carol, she was into sex, all the way…everything. You were her best friend. Didn't you know?"

"She didn't talk much about it," I lied, hoping to encourage Greta to give me more details, the ones I'd never wanted to hear Bethie tell me, but now I would need to know to really understand what happened to her.

"It was hard to talk to her, that's a fact," Greta continued. "After the operation, she was angry at everyone. She said she wanted to come and stay with me, but I didn't want that. She wasn't fond of my three boys and always made that clear. Still, she was very good to me. Paid my doctor bill once…before I had insurance. But I had to think of my family first. Why would I want her to come and stay? Would you?"

"I hope I would have. I'm not sure. So she must have been alone then, from what you say."

"I think not. She told me she was going to call her ex, Reuben Kalig. She mentioned something about wanting his help, though I can't imagine why, since she disliked him so much after the divorce. Did you meet him?"

"No, I never met Reuben, but when she visited me shortly after their divorce, it seemed like she ended up hating him."

"Yes. That divorce was an ugly one!"

"It's hard to believe she wanted to contact him."

"I was surprised too, Carol, but her exact words were 'I'll be needing Reuben's help.' Even at the time, I thought it was strange."

"Didn't she say why?"

"No, and I didn't ask."

At the end of our conversation, Greta gives me Reuben Kalig's address in Springfield, Illinois. "Bethie wrote to me from there before she'd left him. He might still live there, or his mail might be forwarded to him. Let me know if you find out anything." I promised I would, but then she added, "Bethie's final letter really hurt. I really don't much care about her anymore. Bethie could be very cruel."

After talking to Greta, I re-read Bethie's letter, trying to sense some hidden anger in it. I search each line for double meanings and want to cry out to Bethie's ghost for another chance. But it's too late. *She was angry at everyone.* Greta knew. She'd spoken to Bethie several times after she left my house. I must have hurt her more than I thought possible when I let her know I wanted her to leave by asking about her plans. I'd closed the door on any more discussion. If she'd stayed on, we might have come to a new place as friends, but now I can only imagine us maybe sitting in the evening after everyone was asleep, sharing some wine and talking on a kinder, more mature level, even being open enough to discuss our difficult relationships with our mothers. Why did she hate hers? Why didn't I hate mine? Maybe I do. Instead, because of me, we remained locked in the disguised pain of her lonely arrogance and my jealous fear. She didn't write or call me, even when she needed help, and I didn't try to contact her after she left. And now I have to accept some share in whatever caused Bethie's suicide. Greta said Bethie was angry at *all* her friends.

Before she killed herself, did she decide like Van Gogh that we were at least partly to blame, thus seeing us, her friends, as murderers?

She once predicted that in the not too distant future, all conversations would reflect less intimacy. Was she right that even our communication was outdated, that tone of voice and eye contact no longer revealed vulnerability? She believed it would be easier for people not to say what was really on their minds. Reassured by concealed faces and without voices, interruptions and signs, we would all tap messages on the latest typing machines. "No longer immediate responses and no more surprises, just even-toned communications," Bethie said.

"But then," I'd pointed out, "truth or falsehood will require equal amounts of effort, and saved from downcast eyes or from hearing the often broken sounds of emotion gathering in our voices, we'd all just tap on about trivia, anything, without hesitation."

"Exactly!" she'd laughed.

With Greta's input, the best I can do now is try to find out what actually happened to Bethie during those two years after she left our house. We'd shared so much. I have to know more. She would've wanted at least that much from me. I'll contact Reuben Kalig, ask him to visit me, even offer to pay his airfare if he'll come soon.

* * *

"I want to know more about Bethie's death," I write in my letter to Reuben. "The loss of her has left a void in me. We were very close friends once. I always thought we'd become close again some time in the future...."

I show Mark the letter before mailing it off.

"Let him pay his own way," he insists.

"He won't come then."

"How do you know that?"

"I just know. From things Bethie said."

"What good would this do anyway?" he asks, calmer now but still sounding worried. "Come on, Carol, honey, let it go," he urges. He reaches out to take me into his arms, but I move away. I want him to understand how I'm feeling, but that has always been hard for him.

"Let's you and I take a little trip instead."

"Mark. She was my closest friend. I loved her."

"But she's gone, Carol."

"At least now I have to give her some of my time," I insist. "She was so alone while I was here with you and the kids, cooking stew, taking the kids to whatever..."

"Well, I won't let you go loony over this and spend all that money flying him here. It wouldn't be fair. And that's final!"

Suddenly, something between us I've always kept hidden burst from inside of me. Without thinking, I move closer, stare straight into Mark's eyes and say, "I'm going to do this."

His dark eyes open wider, and I feel I'm almost entering them. "This is very important to me," I tell him, and see the corners of his mouth soften to a half-smile.

Soon I hear myself talking with a sureness I'd never before experienced. "Think of this as a business conference I'm setting up," I suggest. "Like some of yours."

"They *are* business, Carol," he says.

"Well, this is now my business."

"The company pays those bills. Remember?"

"I've no company but us, Mark. Who should be paying my bills?"

"Carol, you don't need this. You have the kids and me and the house to look after. Don't look for trouble."

I feel tension traveling from my eyes up to my forehead and my neck and shoulders tighten, and I tell him, "I have to deal with this right now, or everything is going to keep right on going down the drain."

Mark reaches for me and I let him take me into his arms while

I go on explaining, "I have the right to some business like other adults, to make decisions like everybody else, you know." He presses me closer to him and I plead, "Mark, please try to understand. I have to do this for Bethie."

I think now we both realize that my grieving for Bethie has gone beyond what seems appropriate because I'm also mourning for something I've lost inside our life together. "I'm always giving up, Mark. Giving up, giving in, and I'm losing some things important to me. Like Bethie, who suicidally willed me the responsibility to discover what happened to her. I think Reuben knows."

"Suicidally? Okay. Okay, if you want to, invite him to your meeting," he says, "and your company will pay."

Reuben called me a few days later. It might have been after receiving my invitation, which he accepted immediately when I offered to send him a check for the plane fare.

When I tell Mark he's coming, he responds in an annoyed tone, "Why not? After he leaves here, it's a free trip to the beaches, and he can take that looky-loo bus trip to Beverly Hills and Hollywood. Maybe he'll even take in Disneyland."

I don't tell Mark that on the phone, Reuben had sounded strange.

"I am thinking many times I should call Bethie's friend Carol."
"Really?"
"Yes, she told me many times about you."
"Really?"
"She said if anything happens to her, I should call you and

maybe you will help me."

"She did?" I can't help sounding amazed.

"I am looking for a job. I am married again. My wife, Sheila, she is an invalid. I am taking care of her now, but if I find something else, then I will be freer, you know."

"I see." Really I don't, and I'm worried now about inviting him. "Reuben, do you think you'll be able to tell me about Bethie if you come? What happened to her, I mean? That's really what I want to know, Reuben."

"Yes, I will come," he answers quickly. "And I know this because I was living a few blocks from her hotel."

"Then you weren't together again?"

"Yes, together," he insists, "We had plans."

"Plans until she... until she died?"

"I will tell you more when I will see you."

"Well, when can you be here?"

"A week from Saturday, early afternoon. Is okay?"

"Yes. I'll send a check today for the airfare."

The rest of the week, I keep remembering what Bethie shared about Reuben that he probably won't realize I know. *"He's inept... can't even hold a job. I got tired of supporting him."* In another conversation, she said Reuben had used her to get to the States, and when I reminded her of the letter telling me their plans, she said, "We liked playing games like that." Was the divorce part of their games? And why was she back in Springfield with him when she died...and why living in a hotel a few blocks from him? She'd written while in Israel, "Reuben is like me, not religious, and he hates his mother too. Don't we all?" I wanted to write back that I thought the mother-child relationship, while complicated, is often bittersweet, but I didn't. Still, I'd always wondered why she never wanted us to talk about our mothers. Maybe she had scenes like my kitchen scene around the maple kitchen table, coming and fading out, scenes I never wanted to see or mention, fearing they'd explode into my still living, fragile childhood heart.

Was she caged inside her mother's sorrow-filled nights like that one I'd experienced with her? Was she always seeking after the outrageous to mask a painful longing for her mother's love?

My thoughts
unsaid that day,
could they have changed your night?
Oh, was it pain that made your eyes
so bright?

SEVENTEEN

Reuben still hasn't arrived and it's nearly four o'clock. Expecting him at any moment all afternoon, I can't help resenting the hours I waited with not even a phone call to explain. I've just been sitting here on the window seat in the living room, watching neighbors pushing strollers, waving to them and following the way the autumn shadows spread over the lawn and the wind joins fallen leaves everywhere into piles of colors growing taller against fences and along curbs.

Even though he hasn't called, I tell myself, he might be on the way. He could be having trouble finding a cab. More likely, he'll take a bus from the airport. A cab would be too expensive. Maybe I should have sent him more money. Mark and the kids will be home from the movies soon. What a mess that will be--trying to fix us all dinner and having everyone around while Reuben and I try to talk about Bethie. I still haven't told Wendy about how she died. Maybe Mark was right. Sending for Reuben was a mistake.

Just when I'm convinced that Reuben isn't coming, I see a shiny red Porsche pull up in front of our house, and the driver, a well-dressed, dark-haired man who looks to be in his late thirties, walks up our driveway.

It's Reuben Kalig.

"I used your check to drive out in my car." He grins proudly. "Nice, yes?"

"It looks new."

"I keep it nice." He grins wider. "Two years old."

The living room has grown dim and a coolness sets in. I light a lamp and pour us some wine after we sit down in the front room. "It is nice here," he says, "So quiet. But you have some children, no?"

I explain, "Mark has taken all three of them to a children's movie." He asks me more about them and the movie, smiling over the few details I offer. Then I tell him, "They'll be home soon, so let's talk about Bethie."

"That is why I came...and to meet you, too, Carol." He glances at his overcoat that I'd laid across the back of a big chair near the fireplace, then seems to settle down and relax. Taking a few more sips of wine, he sets the glass on the coffee table and starts to talk. "We were married many years. She loved me very much." He pauses, turning to me for agreement, it seems, but I sit stiffly, sipping my wine and deliberately avoiding any comment.

Soon he stands and begins a hasty search in the pockets of his overcoat, then takes out his pipe and tobacco pouch. I watch him fill it and light up. As he focuses on his pipe, I study his very dark, handsome features while his eyes sparkle with charm beneath his prominent, neatly trimmed brows. He appears too well-groomed for someone who has been driving for days. His pin-striped suit and polished shoes look expensive.

Breaking the now awkward silence, I say, "Tell me more about Bethie."

"When she called me, I was getting a divorce from my wife Tina. I told Bethie that in a few weeks more it would be final."

"You had married again then…to Tina?"

"Yes, a beautiful girl from a rich family. Many lawyers. I had to be careful."

"So Bethie wasn't living with you?"

"She was with me." His voice rises sharply. "Staying only a few blocks away in a hotel." In a defensive tone, he offers, "I wanted to help her. We had plans together." He puffs on his pipe with half-closed eyes, his mind seeming occupied with those plans.

"Why did she do it, Reuben?" I press on. "Why did she want to die?"

He takes a few more puffs on his pipe through another silence between us. Then, getting up, he glances around the room. "Ah, yes," he says, standing in front of my bookshelf with his eyes darting up, down and across. He pulls out my small white Bible and brings it back to where I'm sitting, and extends it toward me. "She didn't believe *this* anymore. She lost her faith."

"Because she lost her faith? Did you say Bethie *lost* her faith?" He nods emphatically as if wanting to be sure I understand.

From this moment on, I distrust every word he's saying. Still, I feel compelled to continue with the conversation, even if only to discover what he wants me to believe, so I ask him, "What was she like the last time you saw her?"

"Carol, you will not believe how strange she acted in the hotel." Has he sensed my suspicion? I wonder, and hold a purposely blank gaze as he continues, "I talked to her but she did not listen."

"Did she believe you still loved her?"

"It did not help to say that I love her," he replies with a hint of anger in his voice and a frown.

"Did you?" I dare to ask again.

"You do not understand," he insists. "Carol, she was crazy!"

"Greta Shulberg told me Bethie was very troubled," I say, hoping to encourage him to continue giving me more details about Bethie's state of mind.

"Yes, very troubled. Crying it is no use to live any more. She could not feel my love."

"How did you know? Did she not believe you?"

"I took her to doctors. On the bus. I had no car then. They told her, yes, even after her operations, she can make love, feel it again, but she didn't believe them. She was crying on the bus so everyone can hear that doctors are butchers. I'm telling you, it was no good to talk about love to her. She could not feel it anymore inside."

I stare at him in disbelief. "You mean sex, don't you? You're just talking about having sex."

He ignores me and, his face flushed, he continues. "She burned money. I told her no, don't do this, Bethie, but she burned more, I think to tease me. I grabbed some away. Then she said some of her money is buried in the back of the hotel. She was laughing crazy. I ran outside and around the back to see, but nothing was there, so I ran back, and outside her door, I heard her laughing. I tried to go in but she locked it. I pound and pound, but she would not open the door."

Reuben continues describing the last terrible hours of Bethie's life, revealing how very sick and disturbed she must have been. It's so painful to hear, to believe, but at this point I know he's telling me the awful truth. She had decided she wanted to be alone.

Reuben's focuses again on Bethie's money, telling me, "She saved a lot from her professor's salary. Even when we were married, she gave away money, she said for scholarships to students who can't afford to go to college and to some poor families living in our building."

When I don't comment, he starts working on filling his pipe again, then takes a puff and continues. "After Bethie's funeral, Leona, her mother, came to Springfield to get her daughter's things. She went to the bank with me, and the authorities came to open Bethie's box. No money was left in it. The bank manager showed Leona papers that said Bethie took out all her money from her account a few weeks earlier. For more scholarships, maybe?"

Reuben, focusing on the note waiting for Bethie's mother in the box, looks almost gleeful. "I watched Leona read the note in the bank. Her face turned red and she wouldn't speak to me after. Maybe the note said Bethie is leaving her nothing."

He seems amused, and I can tell he knew what was written in that note. Some kind of game to him that was carried out to the end, and I'm convinced that he played a part in helping Bethie commit suicide. She must have needed him to give her the courage to go through with it. Or was she testing his love by getting him involved, offering him money if he would help her and then waiting to see, hoping he would stop her when she could not stop herself?

Although I despise him for what seems to me his part in Bethie's death, I'm trying to hold back my anger in order to press on for answers to more questions.

"Why did Bethie hate her mother?"

"Because of what happened when her father got sick. He died while Bethie was in Israel. Don't you know?"

I shook my head. *Why hadn't she told me?*

"He was very sick. Leona hired a nurse, left, and moved to her sister in Miami. After he died, they both moved back into the house in Tucson. Bethie was so close with her father, Carol. They loved each other. You knew that?"

I nod, but now I'm confused about what he's saying about Bethie and her father. Was it what I'd thought once when seeing them together? Something I couldn't bear then to imagine, their mutually accepted intimacy in its most subtle form, then perhaps becoming most obvious when she had just started becoming a woman. Since Adam and Eve, with a taste for the forbidden, perhaps all kinds of love have been passed on to us in some erotic mixture of familial pleasure.

Reuben and I sit without speaking, sipping our wine. I'm working hard to stay calm, and I suppose he wonders what to say next. Surely, he senses my contempt for him, though I try to remain civil to keep him telling me more about Bethie before she died. I can only know what he's willing to reveal, and measure that alongside what Bethie had shared with me. And I must keep reminding myself that clearly she had become both physically and mentally ill. That was obvious from Greta's comments, and now from Reuben's as well.

Bethie had always seemed a little crazy. She was so brilliant, so complicated…and then, after planning her suicide and having hatreds to take care of, letters to write, the note to compose and bring to the bank, money to be disposed of as gifts, some by burning for burials or pretended burials, did she promise money to Reuben to help her die and then change her mind? Reuben would never admit to that.

"Who found her?" I ask, breaking a long silence.

"In the morning I went right away for a priest. We came together and we found her."

"Why a priest?" *A perfect cover for him!*

"I knew Father Millcross from my friend Michael's funeral. His church was nearby. I thought maybe he will help her. But it was too late. When we went in, we saw she was already gone. She had the pills, you know, so many. She took them all, they found out after." He shook his head in resignation and got up to pour himself another glass of wine.

"Was the door unlocked?" I ask, deciding before he answers that it would have been if she knew they were coming and waited for them, hoping....

"Yes," he said. "We didn't need to force it open."

The image of the unlocked door and her waiting finally releases all restraints over my emotions. While tears cloud my eyes and fall down my cheeks, he refills my glass. He now hands it to me, perhaps as an offer of sympathy, and says, "You need this, yes?"

I shake my head no as my grief mixes with repulsion for this man who now sits beside me again, seeming to want my understanding of the ordeal he's just described, but when I look at him, I see the opportunist inside this man who has never known a single day of a mother's love, who may have hated her and probably the orphanage that raised him and would have sent him at age fifteen into the army if he hadn't been rescued by some Israelis and later by Bethie. So he did whatever she wanted, learned to play her games with her, taking them on with the seriousness of an occupation until finally they brought each other down to the place where her life ended with him digging for what was left of her money and snatching what wasn't already burned. He must have decided to carry out whatever agreement there was between them, even if it meant... even if it depended upon Bethie dying.

My anger toward Reuben is so overwhelming now, I can feel myself leaning forward toward him while I'm hearing the familiar sound of Mark's car door slam and the children's voices becoming louder as they come up the walk. Quickly, I look away, catching myself on my heels, and, in control again, walk across the room to turn on another lamp.

"Whose Porsche?" Mark calls out when he opens the front door.

"Reuben's. He bought it after Bethie died."

I turn and look at Reuben in time to see his hand clench into a fist before he reaches for his overcoat.

PART III

"Seasoned Bitter and Sweetness"

EIGHTEEN

Long into the night I sit in the memorial candle's faint glow and look back into the parts of Bethie's life I shared, wanting to know more, to understand all that once I'd been afraid to hear her tell me.

On these anniversaries of her death, I call her life back into mine, the tiny flame inside a glass promising to burn fully in the space between two sunsets. It always stays throughout the night and into the next morning when my children notice it, especially Wendy and Daniel, who remember Bethie and ask me about her.

It's possible that I'll never know the real story of Bethie's death. What I now consider to be the truth might someday be disproved, perhaps by some newly discovered type of analysis, computerized with the power to respond more exactly to human emotions and made available to me in my old age as a painful message on a display screen, showing I'd projected my own sense of guilt upon Reuben, thereby judging him unfairly.

Certainly, all the while Reuben and I talked, I felt caught in some terrible dream about Bethie, and I've had many dreams about her ever since.

One begins with a phone call from Bethie.

She is upset even as we talk of routine events. Then she cries out sud-
denly, "I'm sick, Carol, and I've decided to end my life." I'm frightened for
her. I want to help her, but don't know what to do.

"Have you seen a doctor?" I ask. She says yes, that she's seen many doc-
tors. She says she is angry at her mother, who doesn't want her to get help,
that therapy is a waste of money, that she might as well burn it. "Just grow
up, Bethie," she tells me her mother advised.

Soon Bethie is shouting into the phone, "Why don't I just grow up?
Money is my mother's only concern. She doesn't care!" I just listen, not
knowing what to say, and soon Bethie is crying so hard I can't understand
what she's still trying to tell me. I try to calm her, reassure her she can be
helped. I give her names of friends who were helped with therapy.

Hearing this, she stops crying and asks, "Can I come stay with you?"
We both wait for an answer, but it doesn't come. Instead, silence swells
between us.

When I awaken, I'm relieved at first that it was only a dream. Then, upset even more, I reach for Mark to take me into his arms and hold me tight enough to invade that silence; however, he turns the other way.

The next morning, Mark is struggling to control his voice in the kitchen during breakfast, and then in front of our children, he lets us all know why he's angry.

"You've changed, Carol," he says, as if it were a kind of sin. *Yes, and glad of it*, I'm thinking while wedded to my usual silence. Mark stands and leaves the room, slamming the door.

Wendy and Daniel, looking frightened, turn away and run outside to play in the backyard, while Juddy looks at me and begins to cry, then runs to me with outstretched arms. I kiss his wet cheeks, lift his chubby body into my arms and carry him to his room, where we go directly to his bookshelf to find his favorite story about Babar, king of the French elephants. Luckily, we have this peaceful kingdom to go to because Babar's elephant wife, Celeste, is able to maintain her usual, peaceful identity.

Mark is right. I've changed. And for that, I have my friend Jenna to thank. She'd come over for coffee one morning after I'd been up most of the night, trying to recover from another terrible nightmare that returned each time I fell back to sleep. I was too tired and anxious for company, but Jenna had asked to come and return my electric broom.

"I'm not very good company, Jenna. Didn't sleep much last night," I explain. "Having the same nightmare again and again."

"Dreams that keep coming back are important, Carol," she says, sitting down. I pour us both coffee and work at keeping my eyes open and listening to her.

"I once belonged to a dream therapy group."

"Another group?"

"Yes," she laughs. "I learned a lot about how to interpret dreams. I'm pretty good at it now. Try me."

After I down two cups of strong Colombian brew, I tell her the dream I keep having.

"Wendy comes to my bed and whispers for me to wake up and go with her out to the garage. 'There's a cat there, Mom, that needs our help.'

"While she tugs at me to come, I put on a big, black robe

that I think doesn't belong to me, but it's there, hanging over the headboard. Then Wendy and I go down and open the door to the garage and turn on the light. We see a large black cat with shiny green eyes sitting on a piece of old carpet that's stored in our garage. Wendy runs to the cat. 'See,' she points, 'I told you. I think it's hungry. Let's give it some milk.' I agree and she brings a bowl and a pitcher full of milk.

"Wendy keeps pouring out milk as if the pitcher is a magic one, and the cat keeps on drinking until finally I say, 'Wendy, you go to bed. I'll wait for the cat to finish. You have school tomorrow.'

"After Wendy leaves, I move closer to the cat and look inside the pitcher. Nothing is in it. I keep tipping it just as Wendy did, hoping the magic will return, but nothing happens. Then, suddenly, the cat springs at me and attacks my face with its claws. I run screaming for help, my face on fire with pain."

"Is that the end of the dream?" Jenna asks.

"Isn't that enough?"

"Quite!" Jenna's face lights up. "In fact, it's an amazing dream." Without saying more, she gets up and puts the electric broom back in the kitchen closet. "Hmm," she mumbles to herself while closing the closet door. She sits back down, leans her elbows on the table, gives me her most serious look, and says, "Let me tell you what I think, then you tell me if it makes sense to you."

Jenna explains, "Dream interpreters believe that animals often represent some basic aspect of the self wanting to be heard. Your cat was hungry, wanted to be nourished, helped to survive. So, maybe you've neglected some important part of your life, and your dream is pointing that out to you."

"In the garage?"

"Isn't that where the things we put aside are often stored? Like the rug you mentioned."

"But why did Wendy hear the cat first?"

"She's your little girl. Maybe she reminds you of something neglected in you now, or even when you were a little girl. Does this make any sense to you?"

It did make some sense, yet I wasn't convinced until we took up the hideous attack by the cat after Wendy went to bed. "I just can't understand that cat, Jenna. It was so horrible."

"That's the tricky part...though maybe...think in terms of what you've been going through lately. Has something been clawing at you? Frightening you?"

We drink more coffee while I think about what Jenna is saying. Then she adds, "You know, Wendy's leaving could mean it's an issue that you need to face alone."

Jenna's analogies seem jarringly perceptive. When I express my appreciation, it encourages her to persist.

"The real question, Carol, seems to be--what or who is the cat you're unable to nourish? Is she you?"

"The heavy black robe...I'm wondering about that." I'm not ready to pursue Jenna's idea of me with the fangs of some dreadful cat. Could I be that angry with myself?

"What about those poems you started writing when your friend died? Didn't you tell me that when you were in high school you did a lot of writing but now you don't have time? I remember that when I did those sketches for your poems, they seemed very important to you."

Seeing me nodding in agreement, Jenna offers a further analysis. "Carol, maybe your friend's death explains the black robe that didn't belong." Whenever Jenna hesitates, I've learned she's building up her courage to say something difficult for me to hear, so I brace myself with another cup of black coffee as she continues.

"You know, Carol, for a while now, you've sort of been wearing your friend's death, haven't you?"

"I suppose," I admit, bringing my cup down a little too hard on its saucer.

Standing at the door before leaving, Jenna asks me, "Are there any writers' groups around here to join?"

I remind her that my fear of groups hadn't been cured, and instead was reinforced during the San Diego fiasco.

"Well, maybe you just haven't found the right kind of group for you," she replies.

"I'll think about that."

"Good." She pauses at the door. Then, "Carol, you know, I could use another cup of coffee." She comes back to the table and sits down, now with a very serious look.

She stares at her empty cup until I fill it again, and then takes a deep breath. "Actually, I didn't really come to return your broom," she says. "I came over to...well, I wanted to tell you that John left. It's over. He moved out."

"Really? Once before he left but came back."

"Yes, but this time he left for good. When everything is settled, I'll go back to college," Jenna says, trying to smile while adding, "perhaps I'll study to become a paid friend."

"Why not? You're pretty good at it even now."

I pour what's left of the coffee for us and put some cookies on a plate while Jenna talks more about her plans.

"I'll take the kids to Michigan as soon as school lets out. Debra and Mindy love being with my folks and near their cousins for the summer. It'll give me time to work things out."

She's trembling now, and I stand up and put my arms around her from behind her chair and press my cheek against hers. "Hey, it's going to be okay, Jenna," I promise, trying to comfort her, give her hope.

"He's gay, Carol. He's living with his friend, Douglas Mackenzie. I knew they were close. I thought just buddies, especially since John slept with a stewardess friend of mine. What a friend, huh? Anyway, yesterday the kids and I came home earlier than expected from a dinner out and a kids movie, and we found John and Doug in bed together.

"Oh, Jenna. I'm sorry. What a shocking..."

"I'm better off without him," she sobs, pulling tissues from the box I hand her, "but my kids...they still love their pilot daddy."

"He can fly to them for visits, Jenna, and after a while it'll be okay. You'll see."

Before leaving, Jenna, regaining some of her usual self-confidence, forces smiles from both of us when cautioning, "Better get some sleep, Carol, you look awful, and try hard not to let that cat in again."

NINETEEN

After that talk with Jenna, I'm thinking about writing again, and I want to meet other writers, but that idea seems out of reach. Then, I happen to see a notice in our local paper of a poetry reading sponsored by a group called The Circle of Poets.

I call for more information, and a recorded female voice gives me the specifics--time, place, directions, and an invitation to attend at no cost. However, she suggests that donations would be appreciated. The message ends with, "If you're interested in sharing a poem during the open readings, bring ten copies."

I'm definitely not ready for that, but I'd like to attend, even just to see what a group of poets is like.

"Do it!" Jenna orders when we talk about it over lunch. "Go to a meeting at least once, Carol. You need more than kids, shopping and housework, don't you think?"

The Circle of Poets meets twice a week in a room in the old Palm Street Jail, now a rundown red brick building used by various community groups, located just off Palm Street on Waterford Blvd.

The first evening I decide to attend one of their open readings,

Mark is working in Boston, and our usual sitter isn't available. Jenna has found me Heidi, a sitter she often uses. Since little Judd doesn't know Heidi, I'm leaving while he's thrashing and crying in her arms.

Wendy and Daniel must have noticed me rushing them through dinner and prepared for battle. Daniel asks for a second bedtime snack, feigning extreme hunger, and Wendy has turned on the television set upstairs, knowing it's not allowed on school nights. I forgot to tell Heidi that, and I can hear it as I walk down to my car, but I'm not going back. Jenna has it right. I need to go to the readings if I want to meet other poets, hear their work, and maybe someday have enough courage to share mine.

The Palm Street Jail appears to be the next likely prospect for renovation. The parking lot has deteriorated into several broken slabs of concrete lighted by one far-away street lamp. I psych myself into believing it's safe enough to be there because criminal types probably wouldn't want to come near a jail.

No one seems to be around, but I get out of my car, lock it, and hurry up to the paint-peeled door. It opens to lights, the sounds of voices, and two young women seated behind a small reception table in the front entry.

Although they'd never seen me there before, when I sign in, they don't look surprised or that interested.

"Do you want to visit or join?" the thin one with the pony tail asks.

"I'll visit," I say, making an effort to sound casual while hugging my notebook and chalking up my coming there to one more foolish expectation.

When I enter the meeting room, my eyes search nervously for an empty chair in the back row. Seeing one, I dart for it and sit watching as more and more people arrive, mostly in twos and threes, talking to each other as they seek out chairs together.

The room fills quickly, and soon the hum of lively voices fades into quiet as a tall, lanky man wearing fitted jeans and a baggy sweater walks up to the front of the room. He opens the meeting with a few words of welcome, explains the general procedure, and then asks how many plan to read this evening. I hunch down and flip pages in my notebook. Even without planning to read, I feel conspicuously out-of-place.

After these preliminaries, a young blonde woman steps forward and receives a gentle applause. When she begins reading her poem, her voice flows through the room, seeming to reach out to us.

"My poem's called 'Things Given,'" she announces. I look up in surprise, then feel a new excitement as her poem presses hard into my thoughts.

"Once I tried to discard
all things given
to uproot to spit out to remove
even what had been prescribed,
thinking to be the doctor of myself.
But what of the already swallowed?
Still, I did my best,
Studying things given

In mirrors,

In strange exercises

of ceremony and grief."

I weep silently with this young poet as she continues to read my soul into hers, and even before she concludes and sits down to our applause, I know that this is where I belong.

"Our next reader is Seth Brody," a guy with a clipboard announces, and immediately the name brings more audience applause. Then a man's voice calls out from the back corner of the room, "Read 'The Joseph Coat,' Seth!"

"Yeah, Seth, you're on," someone else calls out, then another voice asks for the same poem.

Seth Brody comes up to the podium and shuffles through pages of the published book he's holding. After locating the poem, he smiles and says in a half-joking way, "I'm honored tonight to have written something you remember."

He begins to speak without notes in a very expressive voice:

"The Joseph coat—

it's waiting for one of us,

always one of us

while others watch

the too bright colors of injustice

sting the angry eyes of the disinherited.

I will not open the Joseph coat,

but wear only the vivid threads

of an earned pride.

Let me be one who goes
with brothers and sisters
into the fields of our work
with the blessing of muscled arms,
lifts the heaviest loads
from other shoulders.
When the girl with child on her hip,
When the old one, alone and weary,
When the suddenly sick
call out to us,
I must hurry.
Oh, Father,
burden me no more
with Jacob's foolish gift
to the child of his old age."

Immediate loud applause.

"That was wonderful," I say to the woman next to me, both of us clapping with enthusiasm.

"Yes. We love Seth's work." When the applause fades, she extends her hand. "I'm Christine Thompson, poet and short story writer. And you?"

"Carol Mandell Simon, poet... that is, I write poetry." I feel my cheeks flush in embarrassment.

"It's okay to say you're a poet. You know if you are," she says, smiling. Then, during the intermission, she asks me to join her at the punch bowl and there introduces me to Seth Brody, saying, "This is Carol. She's a visiting poet."

When I extend my hand, he takes it and holds it while welcoming me. "Please come again, and read something for us next time." His handsome, expressive face and his easy smile radiate with genuine interest in me.

The following week, I leave the kids with the same sitter and take off for the poetry readings again. After attending only a few more meetings, I realize that The Circle of Poets is actually a group of very close friends who admire each other's work and see each other to socialize afterward, probably on other nights as well. At the end of each reading, most of them pair off. When I hear them read, it seems to me they're writing and responding to each other with familiarity, even intimacy. While I feel left out sometimes, I'm excited about writing again, and that fire in me lasts from one meeting to the next. For the first time, I'm experiencing the benefits of belonging to a group, but I realize now that the only way I can really hope to enter their close circle someday is by being willing to share my work with them.

* * *

After several weeks of building up the courage to face the evening of my first reading, I feel closer to the group, and I really want to share my cinquains for Bethie, but it'll take another few weeks to secure a place on the schedule. Otherwise, I'll need to be ready for an opportunity at the open readings, which would require an instant burst of courage on my part, still unlikely, but I begin practicing at home the day before each meeting. When I have the house to myself, I stand and recite the five cinquains, at first in tears, and then I say them over and over until it almost seems like somebody else's work.

Finally, when I arrive early enough to sign up for the evening's open reading time, I hear my name called. I walk to the front of the room and stand behind the podium.

"My poem is called Cinquains for Bethie," I say while trying to calm my knees. "It's written in memory of her." Still trembling, and my stomach tight, I breathe into the words of the first stanza and soon hear my voice calling out as if to Bethie's spirit.

"You were
of torch and flame
I only candle light
and yet I walked beside you as
a friend.

Did you
at the crossroad
standing in the darkness
stretch one arm through your agony
for me?

Now gone,
cannot say when
you first saw the dark glare
swallowing you into the mouth
of time.

Was it
one angry wish
or some unsettled debt
to stamp forever on our heads
regret?

My thoughts
unsaid that day,
could they have changed your night?
Oh, was it pain that made your eyes
so bright?"

A loud applause. Then a small chorus of voices in the front row chants my name. I stand there unable to move until Christine guides me back to my seat.

That night I become part of The Circle Of Poets and, in a short time, trust their acceptance of me as a sign of genuine interest in my work. They invite me to join them at the end of our meetings for drinks at Tony's Bar, or for coffee at someone's place nearby, but I always refuse, saying Mark is waiting or that I'd promised the sitter I'd be home early, so they have stopped asking.

Tonight, however, on my way to the parking lot after the meeting, Seth Brody, the handsome poet I'd met at the punch bowl with Christine, approaches me and puts his arm across my shoulder as we walk out to our cars.

"Come join us," he urges. "A little wine, some good music? Come with me to Andrea's? I'll bring you back to your car later." I pull away from him gently.

"I can't. Really, Seth, I have to get home."

"I think you're afraid of us, Carol," he says kindly but disappointed, and it occurs to me then that I *am* afraid, but not only of them...of myself. They seem too free, and I don't know if I can handle that much freedom. Bethie was the only person in my life who, like them, lived in a spontaneous way, unattached, not held back from whatever she wanted to do. People like them sleep with anyone attractive they encounter. They make love because of, or in spite of, or for no reason at all--just because body and soul have the need, and they want to experience all kinds of love. "Free love"-- what most of us turn into fantasy, not daring to let it happen. And maybe it would take some kind of courage to let it happen only once, or the courage to be open and ready for the losses that come with that much freedom. Bethie could handle more freedom than anyone I had ever known, and she is dead. "Not tonight," I tell Seth, "but thanks for asking."

Seth and I lingered after the meeting to talk about the readings, and with much hesitation but with his encouragement, I offered up a poem of mine to him that was too new or felt too close to share at a meeting, and his very gentle, honest response gave me the validation I needed to plan on reading it next week. Then he shared part of a new poem of his.

When Seth read his "Happiness" poem, so perfectly did it speak about me, I had to try to keep from crying until he finished and then run out of the room.

"Happiness, a keen yellow rose
bruised, plucked too soon
withering and falling away
like a young soul abused."

Afterward, Seth found me and brushed my tears away with his fingers, asking why. I pulled away but he drew me close to him and in a gentle voice insisted, "Tell me what you're thinking. Tell me."

"I think of happiness that same, sad way…always fragile, then frail, falling away too soon."

"Still, it's precious," he said, "like love."

Soon the lights in the auditorium go out, and I turn away from Seth. "I've got to go," I say. "My kids are probably still up, waiting for me."

"Of course," he says, "but someday will you come with me? Say when." I choose silence again.

Before I drive away, he stands beside my car and raps on the window, calling out, "I'm going to a party next week. Come with me."

I smile and shake my head no.

TWENTY

Without calling first, Molly drops by in the late afternoon on her way home from what must have been a fancy luncheon, I figure from the way she's all dressed up in a pretty, tailored suit with white collared blouse, and matching hat, purse, and gloves.

After glancing around with a critical look, she chooses a place for her purse, sits down at the kitchen table, and kicks off her high heels.

"Offer me a cup of tea, Carol. I'm parched."

While we wait for the water to boil, Molly tells me about the speaker, what her friends were wearing, and then, as always, she comments negatively about the food. "Awful, as usual. Chefs for banquets have an impossible job. But, happily, I'm dieting, or I would have made a fuss, it was so bland."

While we sip our tea and eat some of the low-fat cookies I happened to buy yesterday, I tell her about my membership in The Circle of Poets. She smiles warily, her usual way of telling me she thinks something I do is ridiculous, and asks, "How much do they raise each year for charity?"

Molly is involved in perpetual fund-raising. Groups need goals,

I suppose, and money is a big motivator. Her clubs actually do a lot of good work for the community, and Molly often serves as their leader. Bob, her husband, knows all the CEOs in the big firms around town. It was Bob who'd recommended Mark for a management position at Astro-dynamics, which brought us to Irvine, where we bought this house in Molly and Bob's neighborhood.

"The Circle of Poets doesn't raise money," I explain while pouring more boiled water into our cups and offering her a new teabag. "We give each other an audience for our writing."

"I thought Dad was your perfect audience," she says in an almost whisper, her face tilted to the side.

"Molly, what is this about Dad and me?" She puts her cup down and stares at me, her arms now folded and her face flushed.

"He always favored you."

For a few long minutes, we just sit drinking our tea and not speaking while I think of the many times I've looked across a table at Molly, my pretty sister, and envied her lovely face surrounded by the blonde hair she inherited from our mother's Lithuanian grandmother. Now in her early thirties, Molly is still a beauty. Hard to believe she has ever been jealous of me.

"Why didn't Dad just come out and say it, Carol?" she asks with hurt and bitterness in her voice. "I always knew anyway."

"He loves us both, Molly. And I know he didn't believe in having favorites. Remember how he'd talk about Joseph's coat-of-many-colors? He said it wasn't right to do that to children. Good parents always try hard not to do that." I almost mention Seth's poem, still so vivid in my mind, but I know she won't appreciate it.

"Impossible not to favor one child, I imagine," she says, "even for parents like you and Dad."

"Maybe so, but at least some try," I say, anxious to talk more to Molly about our parents. "Dad tried, Molly, but Mom never even tried."

"What are you saying about Mom?" Molly snaps back in her stern, older sister voice.

"Only that she so obviously always favored you, and that hurt."

"Mothers always get the blame, don't they?" she says as she gets up to leave and goes for her purse. "I don't have time for this. Have to go, Carol, I'm late for an important committee meeting."

As I walk Molly to the door, she suddenly stops.

"Oh, I almost forgot why I came. How about buying a few raffle tickets for a trip to Israel? It's for a good cause, Carol, and you might win."

"What would I do with it if I did win?" I ask, hoping to sound amused instead of annoyed. "Can I save it for five or ten years?"

"You could sell it. Or better yet, give it to Bob and me. We'd love to go again, and we don't have any kids to worry about," she announces with the same sad note in her voice I hear whenever she mentions her carefree life without children.

"I never win anything, Molly," I say, "but sure, I'll buy a few of your tickets."

I write the check.

As I watch Molly hurry down the driveway to her car, parked at the bottom of our street, I feel sad that we can't talk about anything important to us without getting upset. So much for Dr. Kelly's advice on the benefits of trying that sort of thing. With Molly and me, talking just doesn't work. It always seems as if I'm looking at her from inside some lonely tower--just like now, standing here in front of the window and following her movements while she keeps moving farther away.

When did this feeling start, I wonder, still watching her progress toward her car. Was it our talk about Mom and Dad or... something about her quick, short steps as she moves along the sidewalk? Then a scene flashes in my mind of a time when we lived on Benita Street near the old bus terminal. It was the summer when I was almost five years old.

I see myself again sitting on top of the washing machine with Mom pulling off my hightop shoes and saying I will never have to wear them again when I'm "a kindergarden girl."

Soon Mom is scrubbing my knees, hard...now harder. She's angry at me for dawdling over my dinner while Molly waits out in front for me to finish and come out to play, and then wanders off. Molly, only seven years old, is lost after dark in our neighborhood, one of the worst in town.

"It's your fault, Carol!" Mom yells at me. "She always has to wait for you to swallow down a few spoons of your dinner. You sit there...like a getch. It'll be your fault if anything happens to her." A hard slap across my face is the penalty, then another and a warning of more with her nails digging into my arm as she pulls me down and across the floor. I cry out and then hear my father shouting from the other room.

"Leave her alone, Belle! Get a hold of yourself, for God's sake!"

For a long time, Molly is gone, and I sit looking out of our upstairs bedroom window, crying her name until I see one of our neighbors bringing her up the walk and on to the front porch.

Soon I hear relieved voices downstairs. Molly is safe. They're all happy again, but I'm still afraid.

Twenty-seven years later...still afraid? When will I escape that road bent under our baby footsteps? *Sister, why did you lead me into that darkness part of our mother's heart when she imagined her life without you, her most beautiful child? A part of me still there, looking backward into our young lives, I want to run out, stay closer to you so we'll both feel safe.*

I hear Molly's car start and see her drive off.

Parents...so powerful! A thought too disturbing to dwell on. I leave the window, raffle stubs in hand, then tuck them under a pile of old bank statements and write out a grocery list to take to the store.

A few weeks later, Molly calls to tell me the good news. I've won first prize in the raffle, the trip to Israel.

It turns out that my prize is just one round-trip ticket, but I'm not disappointed. I hadn't planned to go anyway. And I'm not surprised to learn that Calloway Travel was figuring on the probable sale of another round-trip ticket to the winner's companion. When I tell Molly how they'd called and pumped me to buy a second fare, she insists that I'm lucky anyway because I can probably sell mine to someone at a discount. "Or you could give it to me and Bob as payment for all of the babysitting I've done for you over the years."

"Gee, thanks, Auntie Molly."

"Now don't be silly, Carol. I'm kidding. Really, it's a great opportunity for someone who can take advantage of it," she insists, "or just donate the ticket's value back to charity. You know how Dad always said that giving is one of our most righteous acts. Remember you told me that when you wanted to borrow my pink cashmere sweater?"

"You said no, Molly," I remind her, and we both laugh. "Well, anyway, thanks for calling to tell me. I'll think about what I want to do. Maybe I'll just go myself. Every now and then, I do feel like disappearing alone for awhile."

Molly laughs at that, of course, since we can't discuss even potentially troubling ideas like that. Only once can I recall us sharing something rather serious. It happened shortly after we'd moved to Tucson because of Molly's asthma.

Molly and I had come home from school to find Mom at the maple kitchen table, crying into her folded arms.

"What's wrong, Mom?" Molly asks.

"I miss Utica terribly," she says looking up at us, her eyes full of tears. She pulls her handkerchief from the sleeve of her housedress and blows her nose. "I miss my family and friends, Aunt Judy, all her silly ideas. And your grandma. I wish she'd come with us instead of going to the old people's home. I even miss her." She puts her head down again, and we both want to comfort her, but she waves us away.

Later, Molly and I are sitting in the living room together in front of the fan and talking about what to do to lift Mom's spirits. For a while we can't think of anything. Then, I have an idea.

"Let's do something silly to make her laugh."

"It's too hot to do much of anything."

"We can sing 'Dry bones, dry bones....'"

I'm singing it in the deep, southern accent like on our old recording, reminding Molly, who falls off the sofa laughing at me and then decides we might as well try it.

Molly calls out, "Mom, come sit with us near the fan. It's nice and cool in here. Come see." Soon we hear Mom's slow footsteps coming down the hall. When she reaches us, we start singing. "Dry bones, dry bones gonna walk around. Now heed the word of the Lord. Dry bones, dry bones...." When we see her smile, we start laughing so hard we can't stop.

"Enough, you silly girls," Mom orders, but then she's laughing too. Molly and I hug her, and I feel closer to Mom and Molly at that moment than ever before.

TWENTY-ONE

Mark, along with Molly, thinks the idea of joining a group like The Circle of Poets is ridiculous. That may be the only opinion they hold in common.

After I tell Mark about the group, he says, "People who sit around reading personal poems to each other and calling each other poets are silly." When Mark says that, I understand why The Circle means so much to me.

My attendance at meetings makes him decide to go out on those two evenings a week and come back much later than I do.

When his mysterious outings first started, I would shower and wait up for him, stretched out on our firm, platform bed wearing one of my sexiest gowns and silk stockings. Before I fell asleep, I would imagine Mark taking me into his arms the way he used to when we were first married and he wanted to enjoy me. He would try to excite me by touching the deeply hidden soft folds feeling like a closed flower waiting to open between my legs. Then, all too soon, he began to insist on his usual word fantasies and I'd give in to his demands. While yielding, I'd work at imagining myself as one of his favorite prostitutes whom he might soon decide to marry, and soon I'd become excited enough to be taken into the last ravishing moments of our lovemaking. Afterward, I would wonder how this aching singularity of my desire for him could drive me over and over into his arms while, at the same time, my other urgent dreams remained unsatisfied.

On the nights when I waited up for Mark, he usually came home around midnight.

"What were you doing?" I once asked him.

"It doesn't matter."

"It *does* matter."

"What do you do at those meetings of yours? Maybe give each other little hugs? Or maybe you even enjoy some special brand of love only you poets can understand."

"It's not like that. They care about my work."

"What work?" he stabbed, with a piercing testimony of how little he valued what is so much a part of me.

Now when his angry voice echoes its harsh judgment of me over and over, and I realize that my new sense of independence frightens him, I try to seal myself away. Lonely and angry, I wrap myself in extra blankets at night to avoid contact. We still sleep together, but as enemy soldiers assigned to the same bunk.

After another exciting evening with The Circle of Poets, Seth asks if I'll join him at a birthday party that Lila is giving for Christine.

Mark won't be home anyway, I think to myself, so why not?

I leave my car in the parking lot as Seth suggests and drive with him to the party. "I know where they're all going," he says. "Lila and Christine's place. It's not too far from here."

That night I learn that Lila and Christine are lovers. When we walk in, they're holding hands as they sit on the sofa together, and they soon fall into each other's arms. No one seems surprised when they begin to kiss passionately. A few minutes later, they make their way upstairs. It reminds me of the parlor at the UofC dorm on Sunday evenings, where couples would sit around talking, and then, becoming amorous, would leave in search of privacy.

What's next here at Lila's, I wonder, pouring myself a second glass of wine and choosing a few cashews from the bowl of mixed nuts.

Soon Seth suggests we walk onto the patio since it's such a lovely night.

"Are you shocked?" he asks as we step outside.

"No, just amused at how obvious everyone acts."

"Why not? We trust each other."

"I suppose."

"Do you trust me, Carol?"

I nod even though not sure what he really means. He moves closer and kisses my cheek.

"Please don't."

He kisses me again, this time on my lips, and I find myself at first stiffly allowing it, and then returning his kiss.

He notices how tense I am and jokes, "It isn't really a compliment to be trusted by a woman like you."

Seeing my puzzled look, he says, "A beautiful woman like you, Carol? Surely you must know how beautiful you are. A woman cannot be so beautiful and not know it."

"Well, then I'm not beautiful," I answer quickly, the word

beautiful echoing back to my mother's kitchen, where I'd made that final try for an equal share of her admiration and love.

"Why are you so hard on yourself?" Seth asks, and I force a smile, hoping to keep our discussion light. "Your husband must tell you how lovely you are."

"Of course," I say, thinking how Mark had always been more specific. He'd say that he loved my black hair whenever I wore it the way it was when he sang "Black Is the Color of My True Love's Hair" to me. He liked it to simply hang straight and smooth, a few inches below my shoulders. He'd say that way it looked great against a pillow. And when he mentioned my eyes, he'd sing, "the purest eyes and the gentlest hands," ending with the song's last line, "I love the ground whereon she stands."

I never even wanted Mark to say I was *beautiful*. For me, since childhood, that word has been haunted.

"Lately, things haven't been very good between Mark and me," I confide, as Seth and I continue to lean on the patio railing, hearing the music and voices blending inside.

"It happens," he says. "Marriages have a way of going sour, like warm milk, don't they? At least, mine did, and we finally called it quits after a lot of ugly scenes. Why do people wait so long?"

The night sky lights up the patio with its stars, and I feel strangely energized standing here next to Seth, whom I've come to know from his writing on a deeper emotional level than I've ever known with Mark, and that thought frightens me while, at the same time, it fills me with a longing to spend more time with Seth.

"Where are we? What town is this?" I ask, trying to divert us both from the uncomfortable subject of my marriage.

"This is Coral Beach," he says, laughing at me. "When does he let you out, that husband of yours?"

"Oh, I've heard about this place," I laugh. "A lot of crazy artists from Laguna come here, right? And some just plain crazies, too. I hear the strand is full of them."

"Do you believe everything you hear?"

"No, certainly not."

"Well, maybe you should." He kisses me on the cheek. Then, taking my face into his hands, he kisses my lips and whispers, "Believe it. I used to live here and I'm crazy...about you. In fact, I've been crazy about you since the first day you read your cinquains to us, and I always thought of you as...well, as innocent. You know what I mean?"

"Yes." I pull myself from him. "But I'm not."

"I see that now." He pulls me to him again. "You're quite a wise lady. Your poems show that." He hugs me closer and asks, "Does all that knowing make you so unhappy?"

Don't be afraid to be happy, Bethie's voice reminds.

"You aren't happy, are you?" he whispers.

"No. The word *happy* doesn't fit me. It never did."

"Can I try to make it fit?" His eyes, magnetic in their excitement, search my face, while his passionate voice conveys only gentleness. Still, I don't want him to know how much his expressed affection means to me.

"I love your work," I manage to tell him. Your 'Joseph Coat' poem has stayed with me ever since the first time I heard you read it. There's a brave passion in your poems that I love."

"What about the rest of me...the man who wrote them? Do

you want to love him? Will you let him love you?"

"I'm trying hard not to."

"Must you try so hard?"

"Yes." I step away and lean on the rail.

"Why? You said it was over for you and Mark."

"No, Seth. I didn't say that. *You* did."

The crowd inside suddenly begins to gather noisily, and we hear our names called out.

"We should go in," he says, his eyes now downcast. Obviously hurt by what I said, he drops my hand and we walk back inside to sing "Happy Birthday" to Christine.

Later, when Seth drives me back to get my car, we sit in his car for a while talking about the party and how happy it made Christine until our conversation changes to what happened between us out on the patio.

"I disappointed you," I say. "I never meant to lead you on. I'm sorry."

"You didn't. I guess I did the leading."

"Can we just be friends?"

"I probably want you too much for that."

"Seth, please don't," I beg, my eyes filling with tears against my will. "If I weren't married...I'm not free to...you know that. Judaism teaches us to put aside our selfish desires for the sake of others. I know we've never discussed our religion before, but much of your writing reflects your Jewishness."

"Our faith also teaches honesty," he is quick to respond. "It's not a sin to understand our true feelings and express what we want." He turns away, but then looks back at me, and he reaches for my hands and kisses them.

"Tell me what you want, Carol. I know what I want. I've never loved anyone so totally before, and I can't help hoping you feel the same about me."

"I do, Seth, but you're free and I'm not. There's Mark, who I love in a different way, but I still do love him very much. And what about my children? I must think about them first." My eyes flood and I'm trembling now with the realization that I've actually announced to Seth my love for him.

"Carol, I know this is hard for you." He draws me close and holds me until I'm calmer. Then he asks, "Can you give us at least one night together? Just one?"

I shake my head no, tears falling onto his hands.

He kisses my wet cheeks. "A few hours?" he pleads. "Give our love for each other at least that, and I won't ask more of you unless you decide you want that for us."

Don't be afraid to be happy.

"One hour...where?" I hear myself asking Seth.

"I have a cabin in Upper Ojai. It's where I go when I'm working on a book. We could meet there. No problem. It's not a long drive."

"For me to be gone the better part of a day without Mark asking questions is a problem, Seth."

It doesn't take long for that problem to be solved.

On Wednesday evening, Mark announces that on Friday, he's flying to Boston for a business conference and he'll be staying over until Monday.

"The whole weekend?" I ask. "You usually return on Saturday."
He doesn't answer. I try to stay calm while questioning him again
about his plans. "So you don't plan to return until Monday?"

He gives me a blank stare and goes to get his suitcase out of the
downstairs closet.

Mark's silence hurts, but I'm guessing his reason for staying
away longer would hurt even more, so I let it drop.

How easy now for me to go to Ojai and be with Seth without
Mark knowing. But could I ever really do that? *Don't be afraid to be
happy.* Is Bethie's spirit urging me on? Has she become a part of
me now?

A few hours. That's all Seth is asking of me. Even in the first year
of our marriage, Mark insisted he should always have the kind of
sex he needs. What I wanted was never enough to make him happy,
and I began to wonder if with someone else, I might experience a
deeper intimacy.

Maybe with Seth....

I decide to meet Seth at his cabin in Ojai on Saturday, and
soon I'm planning what to wear. I lay out my shortest narrow
skirt, a silky, lemon-colored blouse, and the pair of emerald
green, dangling earrings that Bethie gave me for my birthday. I'd
thought they were too obviously sexy then, but kept them anyway. I try them on and wonder if Seth will like how I look when
he sees me wearing them.

TWENTY-TWO

The last few miles of my trip to Upper Ojai has become a panorama of peaceful green farms with a few healthy-looking horses trotting about, orchards separated by stands with boxes of oranges and strawberries in front, and then hilly streets with neighborhood markets and diners come into view.

Seth's cabin, peeking out from the surrounding trees, sits on one of the hills far back from the road. I park below and walk up to it while noticing him watching from the large front window and then disappearing to welcome me at the door.

He has been here overnight, and I suspect he has spent some time getting ready for me since the place is fairly neat. Although sparsely furnished, the three small rooms look very comfortable.

We stand together in the tiny front room hugging, then sit down on the wood-framed futon, which takes up nearly half of the room. The other half is devoted to a large desk, a bookshelf, and a file cabinet.

On the wall over the sofa, I'm delighted to see that Seth has hung a large, framed copy of Klimt's most famous painting, *The Kiss.*

"I've spent many weekends writing here," he says.

"I can see how it would be a writer's perfect getaway. No television, no phones."

"Hey, you look great in that blouse, and those earrings are very sexy." He takes me into his arms.

"I wanted to be here earlier," I confess, "but couldn't get a sitter until noon. Luckily, my friend Jenna recommended someone available until seven this evening."

"Just until seven?" His face falls in disappointment.

"I'm sorry, Seth. I'll have to leave by five. But I'm here now," I remind him.

He makes an effort to smile and asks, "How about something to drink? My friend Carl lives up here year-round. Brews his own beer and keeps me well stocked."

"Sounds good." I watch him reach into his small refrigerator for a bottle labeled Carl's Brew and two chilled mugs. "You're a planner, I see." I choose the one poured with the most head. "I like the foam on top. My dad always poured his beer that way."

After toasting brewmaster Carl, we drink our beers with our attention turned toward *The Kiss* hanging on the wall behind us. Klimt's most famous painting, often described as a monument to joyous, pure love, shows a dark-haired man wearing a long, jeweled robe, within which he embraces a woman whose eyes are closed in a peaceful expression of quiet ecstasy.

"It's one of my favorites," I tell Seth. "His coat...it's like a Joseph coat, isn't it?"

"Amazing! I thought that too." He leans over and brushes his lips gently against mine, and then we kiss like the couple in Klimt's painting.

We take our beers to the kitchen counter and sit down on the tall, backless stools.

"If I could open the Joseph coat and keep you with me just like the guy in the picture," Seth says, "I'd wear that coat forever."

"No, you wouldn't," I tease. "Remember, in your Joseph's coat poem you said you wouldn't wear it? But did you ever want to wear a special coat like Joseph's when you were a boy?"

"Well, maybe for a little while."

"Who offered it to you?"

"My father. But his love came with a lot of heavy expectations I didn't want to fulfill."

"My sister Molly likes being my mother's favorite."

"What about your genius friend, Bethie?"

"She liked her father giving her all his love and attention. Probably too much for a little girl. *Now you're all we have.* After a while, I think it dragged her down. However, like Joseph's many-colored-coat, Bethie's father gave her the gift of a dazzling sense of herself."

Seth nods. "That kind of power, when exaggerated, can be dangerous." He pulls me up and again drapes himself over me as in *The Kiss.* "Or it can be quite wonderful."

Still embracing, we walk into the tiny cabin's bedroom. The double bed takes up most of the space. We have to take turns walking around it to get to the small tables and lamps on either side. We laugh about that while undressing, and I notice how much he resembles my fantasies of the biblical warrior and singer of psalms, King David. "Seth, I love looking at you," I murmur. He reaches for me, and with his muscular arms revealing their strength, he carries me to the bed.

Both now lying naked together, Seth announces, "I love looking at you too." He studies my breasts and thighs with his fingers and then massages every part of me, and I come alive with pleasure until I'm aching inside for him to press his flat stomach against me and envelop me with his passion.

All afternoon, we laugh and cry and sing to each other before each feverish embrace, and I never close my eyes once to fantasize or hope for stronger, more demanding words to help me climax. Instead, I'm silently reciting from The Song of Songs. *My beloved is mine, and I am his....*

In this quiet moment after our lovemaking, I wonder about the ease of our intimacy. Were we meant to be together? But how could that be? I thought that too about Mark and me. Now, with thoughts of Mark invading, I push them aside by telling myself I have the right to this kind of intimacy with Seth, who can enjoy me in a way that makes me feel loved.

"Are you happy, my girl for an afternoon?" Seth asks, as if he knows what I've been thinking.

"Oh, yes." *Happier than ever before.* We spend our last hours together feeding each other grapes along with tiny bits of cheese, and alternating between making love and reciting poems.

"As soon as I saw you that first night when you came to the poetry readings, I knew you belonged there," Seth says as he pins behind my ears the tresses of damp hair from my cheeks.

"Really? That's amazing!"

"Something about the way you sat there at the back of the

meeting room, perched on your seat like a hungry young bird just waiting to be nourished. I had an intuitive impulse then to be the one to capture you and keep you with us."

I laugh and push back the strands of black hair from his forehead, and in this moment, he's everything to me--son, brother I never had, father, lover, all erotically fused again into my David the King images while Seth continues the saga of our first meeting.

"I even selected a poem that first night to seduce you. But then my friends began chanting for the Joseph Coat poem, and my plan seemed lost."

"Poor Seth." I kiss his cheek. "Tell me the poem."

"It's called 'Seasoned.' You know, I'm a lot older than you. Ten years, at least."

"Really? You look wonderfully young."

"I'm seasoned well then. I want you to hear how it is for me now and how it might be for you someday too. It begins:

"Seasoned, I talked to the spring,
said come to me, jade eyes with flowers
just as you did before,
heard her refusal in leaves
whispering against a stone wall."

"I already know how that feels, Seth. I'm not that young," I remind him, though happily flattered, and I feed us another bunch of grapes.

When we finish, I tell him, "I wrote this poem on the day I turned thirty:

"Wild Things in me
sacred and backward dreams
danced out for a while,
now what to do with them?
Help me, dance-spirited mother of myself,
help me to know what to do with them."

"I know what to do with them. Come here, wild one."

He pulls me closer. "I love you, Carol. Today you're my joy, but tomorrow? Then you're my sadness."

"I'm feeling sad too because..." *I want to say because it'll never be the same when I go home to Mark.* "...soon I'll have to leave you."

Seth fits his fingers into mine. "My sadness will always be because there will never be a child of ours. I want you to have our love child."

"Seth, please. We agreed not to let that happen. But I'll always remember this day when my soul danced only for you."

"Dance for me again then, and let's toast to our forbidden love."

Forbidden. The word startles me back to reality.

"I have to leave now, Seth." I turn away from him and reach for my clothes, but soon feel his strong arms circle my waist, and I stop moving to capture a few more precious moments.

* * *

Mark is still away when I return home with my wedding vows echoing back my broken promise...*keeping yourself only unto him? I do.* And now I've come to know the pain that inhabits the forbidden, the unending mixture of excitement and fear it thrives on.

While hardly able to keep myself from running into my bedroom and throwing myself weeping onto the bed, I go about fixing dinner, helping the children prepare for bed, and listening to the quiet chatter about their day with the sitter.

Later, I feel some relief when Wendy offers to read the boys their usual bedtime stories. Straining for a calm voice, I answer, "That would be nice, Wendy."

Daniel agrees, saying, "She's the best big sister in the world. She gave us lots of ice cream last time when she read about the penguins."

When the children fall asleep, I let myself weep while hiding my face in pillows so I don't frighten them. At the same time, I'm remembering the cries of Bethie's mother that night I'd spent at her house, unable to keep from hearing the sounds of her deep grieving, probably for her son, Alex, and maybe also for his father. Did she try to hold back her tears, as tonight I waited for the darkness to release mine? But her pain would not go away. She'd still never found comfort and strength. Hers was the worst pain of all, losing a child. I can't even imagine.... She must have known we could hear her sobbing. What mother would want to do that if she could stop herself?

Seth's love for me and mine for him, all its unbounded, awesome beauty that afternoon, is now enjoined with fear, and I'll never risk for it again. I must not let my loss spill into my children's lives, damaging them like Bethie's mother surely must have damaged her.

Later that night, I feel comforted for a little while by whispering the words of a healing song I learned at a retreat. "Help me find the courage to make my life a blessing, help me...." And soon after, I hear Bethie's confident, clear voice reassuring me again that I have what to takes to be strong. *You have what Tillich calls rare moral courage. People like you know when the most essential aspects of life must prevail.*

In the morning, when I come downstairs a little later than usual, I find Wendy sitting on the bottom step. She looks worried.

"Mom, are you okay?"

Was she standing at my door last night? Did she hear me weeping? Maybe not. Please God, maybe not.

"I'm fine, Wendy," I tell her, hoping to hide my true state of mind. I pull her up and hold her tight against me. She throws her head back and searches my eyes. I kiss her cheek and then the tip of her nose. She giggles and runs off to eat cereal and watch cartoons with the boys.

"Don't worry," she calls back. "I'll pour their milk, so they don't make a mess like last time."

For a while, I listen to Wendy chattering with her brothers as she serves them breakfast. She's strong like Bethie, not like me. Will I always be a weeper by night and a silent sufferer by day, like Bethie's mother?

I can't let that happen!

Part IV

"Jerusalem"

TWENTY-THREE

The children and I have just finished a picnic lunch of leftovers for me and their favorite, peanut butter and grape jelly sandwiches. Now they're running around the yard playing tag. I'm loading things onto a tray to bring inside when the kitchen phone rings. I stop and hurry in, pick up the receiver, and soon hear the very unexpected voice of Reuben Kalig.

"Carol, I am in Santa Barbara," he announces, "at my brother-in-law's. He is handling my wife's estate. She died a month or two maybe after I visited you."

"Oh, I'm sorry to hear that," I say while thinking how strange it is that another wife of his is gone, and I'm wondering why he's calling me.

Reuben explains, "I'm staying not far from you, in Santa Barbara, but soon I'm leaving for Israel, and before I go, I want to see you again, tell you more about Bethie." A pause. "I think I will stay in Israel."

My mind races with hopes of having a last chance to learn more about Bethie and, even if for only a day, have time away from my troubled marriage. I'm not sure how Mark will react or whether he will even care if I go to Santa Barbara to see Reuben.

In order to know more about what happened to Bethie, I need to talk to Reuben again.

I tell him I'll come, that he can expect me there by late afternoon. Santa Barbara is about a two-hour drive from Irvine, and I'm almost certain I can get a sitter.

"We will have dinner together then, Carol. Yes?"

I agree and he gives me his phone number.

Now I must turn my attention to facing the very unpleasant task of talking to Mark about my plans. He has been coming home late from work every night.

During dinner, Daniel keeps asking for his daddy. "He used to read us stories and play Hop-on-my-back." It breaks my heart when I see him waiting near the door before dinner and then staring sadly at the empty seat at the table. Wendy knows things aren't good between Mark and me, but she doesn't ask anymore now that she's moved into the peer culture at school, and little Judd, who hardly knows his daddy, is clinging to me as if Mark isn't part of the family. When I bring this up, he just stares at me as if to say it's my fault for not being a good enough wife so he'll want to come home to have dinner with his children.

I call Mark at his office and tell him my plan to go and to find a sitter who can stay with the kids until he comes home. "I'll take the coast route to enjoy the view," I add, "make it an adventure as well. This may be my last chance to learn more about Bethie from Reuben."

"Don't go!" Mark orders.

"I'll be back tomorrow morning," I assure him, somewhat relieved by his obvious concern.

"You'll stay over with Reuben?"

"No. I'll find a place up there to stay so I won't have to drive home late."

"Sure," he replies in a doubting tone.

"Do you really think I'd stay with Reuben?" I laugh at the idea, but he doesn't.

"I don't trust that guy. Neither did you...that is, until now."

"I need to go, Mark." I try to explain, "He'll soon be leaving for..."

"That's it, Carol. If you go, that's it!"

With my heart pounding, I shout back, "How about your mystery nights and the weekend trip? You won't even tell me..." A click at the other end of the line. Mark has hung up on me. Another ugly first. What's next, I wonder in tears.

Still upset, but determined to go, I consult my list of sitters and begin calling until I reach Maggie Carlow, one of Jenna's sitters, who is willing to come within the hour and stay overnight if necessary. Explaining and having to work around Mark's absences is difficult and humiliating, but I've learned to handle these situations by compiling a list of trustworthy sitters. Still, they must realize things aren't ordinary at our house. I worry they might talk about that with the children, ask questions that will upset them.

"It's very possible," I inform Maggie, "that Mr. Simon may not be coming home, and if he does, it might be only for a short time. He might leave again, go out of town like me for the night." Maggie looks a little puzzled, but she agrees to stay over if necessary. She says when she babysits, her mother has agreed to be available in case of an emergency.

I'm driving north along the coast highway toward Santa Barbara, glancing often at the sparkling blue Pacific at my side while I try to recover from the phone conversation with Mark before I left. Still early in the afternoon, the traffic is light enough for me to relax now, view the shoreline, and think about meeting with Reuben again. Certainly, I decide, there'll be no stopping me from asking about Bethie and him during those final days of her life since this time, he has contacted *me* even after our difficult last meeting and is saying that he wants to tell me more. I never thought I'd hear from him again, but now I'm determined to find out all I can about Bethie before he leaves for Israel. I can't allow Mark's threat to keep me from doing that.

I drive on, holding back tears but taunting myself with the reality of what has happened to our marriage. Wasn't it all over anyway before today? Our happiness together, like china cups breaking one after the other until we'd even stopped wanting to have tea. Since losing Bethie, everything changed.

After another crying jag, I manage to pull myself together and get through the traffic around the LA airport by focusing on the reason for the trip and the phone call from Reuben. He sounded strangely energized this time...maybe excited about going back to Israel. But without any family there or a job waiting? Seems like a strange decision. And what about his late wife's estate? Was Reuben up there in Santa Barbara with her family because she left him some money? Enough to pay for his return to Israel? Maybe he sold the Porsche. With that money, no doubt Bethie's money, he could make a fresh start. But was that what she wanted? There is still so much I'm hoping to learn about Bethie from Reuben.

I continue along the Pacific Coast Highway as the sun peeks in and out of trees and tiny beach towns, until I arrive in Santa Barbara. Then, I take a downtown freeway exit and head for a side street, where I see rows of what look like recently built apartment buildings. Who would want to live here, I wonder. Then I consider the possibility of people just happy to have a new place to rent not that far from the beach, but who don't realize that the nearest post office probably needs caged windows to keep their employees safe. After finding street parking, I work on deciphering my erratic handwriting for the address Reuben gave me and study the street map until I think I can get to where Reuben is waiting.

As soon as I pull up in front of the small, shabby downtown hotel with the address Reuben gave me, I think maybe Mark was right. This dingy, backstreet hotel is not a place where I want to spend even an hour alone with Reuben. I check the address a third time and read the three numbers on the cracked front sign announcing "Holiday House." Having been so surprised by his call this morning, I hadn't thought to ask him anything about the place where we'd be meeting. He'd said he was staying at his brother-in-law's home. I didn't know this hotel was his home.

As I slowly venture from the car, gruff, arguing voices are coming from the nearby alley. The hotel itself seems deserted except for Reuben, who I now see standing in one of the doorways. He immediately hurries toward me, frantically calling out, "Carol, wait!"

When he's standing next to me, I smell alcohol on his breath. He urges, "Carol, come. I'll show you around my brother-in-law's hotel." He takes my arm and leads me into the lobby. "You can stay here tonight if you want." He continues walking me in while explaining, "I have an apartment here until I leave."

Nodding to the young room clerk as we pass the front desk, we proceed toward an ancient-looking elevator at the end of a hallway. "Albert and Ellie, she is his wife, will give us some dinner later at their place," he says. "Ellie makes good corned beef and cabbage."

Hearing about Ellie relieves my anxiety a little as Reuben closes the iron-railed door of the old elevator and presses the number four button, which starts the lift groaning in labor as it rises.

"A nice room they have for you here," he says.

"I'll decide later," I answer, hoping to sound in control. Having seen Reuben only the one time at our house, I'd imagined he would look the same way, a little overdressed and unsure of himself, but today, he looks so different. Dressed in casual clothes, he appears physically strong, like men who work out all the time in gyms or do heavy labor. His large bulging arms look hard and veiny. His craggy face is still as handsome as I remember it, but he's much more anxious, and his eyes now seem to have the intensity of a stare.

All this worries me, but I'm usually fearful in new experiences, and I've learned not to trust my first impressions. So, even as I now suspect another side to Reuben, I admonish myself to "grow up" in that same harsh way Bethie's mother advised her in one of my dreams.

Reuben, keys in hand, struggles to unlock the door. He finally manages to open it for us and smiles with new confidence. I immediately realize how naive I've been to assume we'd soon be on the way to Albert and Ellie's apartment for dinner when, standing in the doorway, he announces, "I have prepared some wine for us here, Carol, in my apartment, so we can talk."

Once in, my eyes scan the ugly grey cracked walls and stained carpet while I'm searching for any comforting sign, but I don't see any. Now it seems I've been summoned by some unrelenting force to this dingy room, where Reuben clumsily pours two glasses of red wine from a cloudy glass pitcher. He places them on opposite sides of an old folding table between two wooden chairs. I wonder what kind of wine it is, but don't ask. I sit down in the chair across from Reuben and, almost touching his carelessly made bed, I feel energized by fear as if, sitting opposite of Reuben at the table, we're inside a ring of fire with no alternative but to fight to the bitter end.

Having come to listen to what I'd always been afraid to hear, I sit stiffly, leaning forward slightly and sip the wine, hoping it'll calm me. Reuben gulps down his and pours himself another glass. He drinks that, then, pouring himself a third glass, he begins to talk about Bethie in a vengeful tone. I tighten my grip on the edge of the table.

"Bethie could be very cruel." He bends closer across the table, his words slurring. "She needed a man who was strong like me... strong enough to take care of all her very special needs, Carol. You know what I mean?"

I nod quickly, hoping that stops him from saying more. Never had I asked for details about Bethie's sexual encounters, fearing what she would tell me. *I want to experience everything.* But now, sitting in that room with Reuben, I'm listening to familiar echoes of the past heightened to a new intensity by Reuben's suddenly raunchy tone. "Oh, yes, Bethie's good friend Carol, you and I know about women having their own special needs."

I sit there stunned by his words until, maybe to arouse me, Reuben labors to stand, and then, bending over me, exclaims, "Yes, Carol, she wanted me to play her games. I gave her the kind of love she needed and the other kind she also wanted...to be in charge." My face flushes with helpless embarrassment as he grins like a jack-o'-lantern, saying, "But you know about her little games, Bethie's good friend Carol, the kind she liked." He reaches down and starts to unbuckle his belt.

I jump up, knocking over the table between us, and I shout out, "Punishment!" The word bursts out of me with such force, it causes me to stumble a step toward him.

Reuben backs off, and now I realize my sharpest weapon against him is the pitiful, unrelenting truth, no longer to be denied, and with my fear energizing me, I continue my assault. "Punishment!" I shout out again, whipping him with the word. "You and Bethie played punishment games, didn't you, Reuben? Maybe even right up to the day she died? Wasn't that it? You played your sadistic, painful games?"

He shakes his head no, but his eyes grow wet with what I see as guilty agreement, and I continue torturing him as if nothing else matters.

"Even Bethie's death might become part of a game for you, right, Reuben?" And again his eyes are telling me I've come close to the truth. "And you, of course, would win the final round because

Bethie was really too sick to play her part. But Bethie was always very brave, so she must have played it out anyway, right to the end. You knew she would, and you could then gather up what was left at the end. Wasn't that your plan?"

His face is flushing a deeper red as he backs farther away from me, but I lunge more forward to insist that he hear everything I feel compelled to say.

"Now I understand what happened--Bethie and you finding each other, each becoming the other's victim. That's how your games were played."

When he's pressed against the wall, I stop moving toward him and continue to attack his soul, charging without mercy, even beyond what I know is fair, but I'm unable to stop myself.

"Bethie usually won, didn't she, Reuben?"

He stares at me without answering, his lips, closed tight at first, are now trembling.

"Yes," I nod with assurance, "that's why she decided to divorce you. It wasn't any fun for her anymore. What was it she called you? Inept! She told everyone you were inept. You must have hated her when she left you."

"No." His eyes are welling up with tears and his body is trembling, but he manages to tell me, "I never hated Bethie. She loved me until she got sick and could not love me anymore."

"Still, Bethie was the strong one, Reuben, and she could be cruel. You said that, and her friend Greta said that. But she was always kind to me even though I didn't play her games because... well, because, thank God, I was afraid of them!"

"Carol, you were the one she loved most. Bethie was always

telling me that."

His words, seductive in their calm, hang in the air like a string of pearls held out to me, and I want to grasp them and wear them forever.

"I loved her, too," I murmur. "We were close."

"I know, so I'm thinking you two must have…"

"You thought wrong. I loved her like a sister."

He gives me a puzzled look, still not seeming to understand the usual bonds of family life, but I try again. "We were close like sisters…like a parent and child."

"Like Bethie and her father? *That* way?"

"What do you mean *that* way?"

He shrugs, then kneels down and begins picking up everything that had dropped off the table when it hit the side wall. I watch him wipe up the wine spills across the tabletop with the wads of paper napkins he's pulled out of a cabinet drawer.

Soon the two unbroken glasses stand empty in their original places on the table, and we sit down again. Reuben offers to pour me more wine, but I shake my head no, and he pours what's left for himself.

I'm exhausted from the ordeal and wondering if I can make the drive home, but I'm afraid to mention his idea of having dinner with Albert and Ellie, and I don't want to stay. I don't even feel like talking anymore.

"Reuben, I need to leave before it gets dark. I want to get home in time to put my kids to bed."

He, however, is determined to tell me more about what happened to Bethie and Alex.

"It was what she wanted," he says, "to play games like with Alex. She playing them with him until he said he wanted to hurt her. Then she was afraid of him. But their games, she still wanted. So I did like Alex. We played the games she played with him."

"Why would Alex want to hurt her?"

"A boy fifteen years old feels like a man. I was fifteen and ready for the army if I hadn't left Russia."

I nod, reminded of Daniel, who just turned thirteen and is already showing signs of his growing manhood.

"I am telling you, Carol," he continues, "like Bethie told her parents, Alex wanted to hurt her. But she told me she was still willing to play their games. Even though she was afraid of them."

I shake my head in disbelief.

"Yes, Carol. She ran from him and hid from him until her parents came home and found her in her bedroom closet. She said she thought it was part of their game, but it scared her."

"Poor little thing. She must have been so confused." I close my eyes to blot out that whole scene and to keep from crying.

Reuben continues on. "If she didn't run, who knows what would have happened. Leona wanted to take Alex to see a doctor, but Meyer insisted they send him right away to his uncle in Paris. Leona finally agreed to ask the uncle to let Alex stay with him for a while, and he agreed. But a few months later, Alex died there while at his new school during some games."

"Did they know how he died?"

"A heart attack. Bethie said her father told her that Alex had a heart problem they didn't know about. But her mother blamed Meyer for sending him away, and she blamed Bethie, too, and wouldn't talk to her for a long time."

"How could she blame Bethie?"

"Mothers!" He looks away, then back at me with his face etched in some kind of pain I've never seen before. Then he forces a smile to tell me, "If Lena, a worker at the orphanage, had not cared for me, I maybe would have stopped breathing like what happened to many babies who came there."

"Sounds like marasmus, a disease that's common in very young babies given too little mothering."

"But Lena wouldn't let me go to them when they cried. She said I'd get into trouble, and I knew to always obey her so she would look out for me. And she did, until I was nine years old. Then she got transferred somewhere else. I cried a long time for her after that, but she never returned."

"That must have been so hard, Reuben, growing up there, never knowing your parents."

"Yes, I was told only that they were enemies of the State. Lena thought maybe they were sent to Siberia."

Reuben talked more for a while about the orphanage, about Lena, his caretaker, and the potato soup they gave him daily, which he'd come to despise so much that ever since he left Russia, he has never eaten a potato.

"Not even French fries?" I joke, but he shakes his head no, without smiling.

"But then, in Israel, Bethie helped me with my studies, many things, and then she married me so I could come with her to America. Yes, she loved me very much then."

The late afternoon light is growing dim while Reuben talks on, seeming now willing to tell me even more about what happened during his last few weeks with Bethie just before she died.

"Bethie called and asked to come see me. She said she needed my help. I told her yes, but it is not a good time, that I am waiting to hear the reading of my wife's will. She came anyway and stayed in a hotel here."

"How did she get sick, Reuben?"

"Not from me. From others. Many others, Carol. She was first sick with gonorrhea, but she was ashamed to go to the doctor. It got worse. Spread. Then there in the hospital, she got another infection. She had so many operations and so much pain."

"Why didn't she protect herself?"

"She thought she knew what to do. Bethie always thought she knew."

I know how to take care of myself.

I nod, sadly remembering her proud announcement.

Reuben gets up and turns on the pole lamp near the table, and then continues. "When she visited you, she said she borrowed your car to see a doctor, who ordered tests and gave her more pills. Even then she wasn't feeling good, and the doctor didn't know what was wrong with her."

"She seemed healthy, and she looked so lovely. She even went out with a guy Mark invited to dinner to meet her, and they stayed out all night."

"She didn't tell you she wasn't okay?"

"No. I guess I didn't give her a chance. She only stayed a few days. We argued, and she left the next day. If only I'd known. I feel so ashamed."

Before getting up to leave, I ask Reuben, "Are you really going back to Israel?" *Hard to believe he'll leave his in-laws if there's any possibility of money for him.*

"I want to go to Hebrew University and bring a copy of Bethie's thesis, the one she wrote first in Hebrew. She was going there on the bus two or three times a week until...until the kibbutz told her to leave."

"Why did they tell her to leave?"

"Rules were to break, she thought. But not there, not at Kibbutz Kavodim."

"Was that really why she left?"

Ignoring my question, he seems determined to tell me more about Bethie's thesis. "She said her thesis belongs to the kibbutz because she wrote it while she lived there and they paid for her to go to Hebrew University. Bethie decided that if it was published, any money that came from it should go to the kibbutz."

"How can it go to them?"

"I don't know, but before she died, she asked me to promise her that when..." He stopped himself.

"When what?" *So they did plan for when....*

"If anything happened to her, I promised to tell Rabbi Micah Stern. He is the professor whose wife helped me when I came to the university from Russia. Rabbi Stern was Bethie's thesis advisor, and I met Bethie in his home. Mrs. Stern invited us for Shabbat dinner. Before Bethie died, she told me Rabbi Stern will know what to do when he sees me, and he will recognize me. He knows

only my Russian name, Kalig, the name they gave me at the orphanage. When I came to America with Bethie, I gave myself a first
name, Reuben, and a last name, Kalig. Bethie liked that. She said a
new name for a new start in a new country is good."

I finally brave my last question.

"Where did Bethie get enough pills, Reuben?"

"I helped her to get some. I had a friend who worked in a phar-
macy, and Bethie was crying to me, 'Reuben, I am so tired. I don't
sleep. I need pills to help me sleep.'"

He drops the pill subject and then goes on to say, "She was even
telling me she hears a child calling her."

"Reuben, Bethie said she didn't want children. I don't believe..."

"She wanted what she could not have."

A longing for the forbidden. We both know about that now, Bethie.

"I'm telling, you, Carol, she wanted a child. She was saying if
only she had a little girl like Carol's or a boy to name for Alex."

I get up, and moved now by knowing more about his difficult
childhood, I extend my hand to him. He takes it in a tender way. I
squeeze his hand. "You're a survivor, Reuben. I'm glad you're going back to Jerusalem, the city of redemption."

"Maybe not for me, Carol," he replies. "In this country, you
know how they say you can't go home again. Besides, I will need
money to go. First I must see what will be with my brother-in-law
about Sheila's estate. If not money from there, then maybe I will
get it somewhere else. Maybe a job, or..." He leans toward me,
asking, "Do you think, Carol, your husband would loan me the
money, or could he find me a job?"

When I shake my head, he suggests, "Then maybe you could

loan me some money, or maybe...." He is now beginning to plead with me. "Go with me, Carol, to Jerusalem. Please. You are a very pretty lady, and you came to me here. You and I could..."

"Reuben, stop!" I pull my hand away.

He smiles, looking only a little embarrassed. Then he admits, "I don't know if I can. This country, it is full of women who have money and need a man like me, and they are happy to pay, Carol."

This unexpected honesty is shocking!

"Bethie, too, then," I say.

He immediately begins to weep, and it sounds like something is breaking inside him. I press my hand over his again until he calms down.

Reuben soon recovers and gets up to make a pot of coffee, and both of us sit waiting for the coffee without speaking. When it's ready, he pours us each a cup, and I break the silence by suggesting, "When you go back to Jerusalem, Reuben, don't expect to find what isn't there. Look for what's different. Plan for something better. Maybe a family of your own."

He nods, seeming to connect with what I'm saying.

"And if you need help to go back, Reuben, and to bring the original copy of Bethie's thesis to Rabbi Stern, I know someone who will be able to give you a plane ticket."

Surprise and then relief spread across his troubled face, and he says, "*Toda*," the word for thank you in Hebrew. Then he smiles and adds, "Bethie told me if ever I need help, maybe you will help me, Carol."

I want to tell him that I don't believe Bethie said that, but I let it pass, extend my hand to him and say, "Shalom, Reuben. I'll call you soon about the ticket."

While riding down in the trembling elevator, I can't help but wonder if my offer to give Reuben a free ticket to Israel was such a good idea.

TWENTY-FOUR

I begin the long drive home, and all the while, it seems that Bethie's spirit is traveling with me, still with enough force to have caused me to make this trip earlier in daylight and now back in darkness. Perhaps someday the dead will be tracked in some way that will reveal their actual pathways in and out of our lives, and we will talk of them all--the roots and stems of us, flowers fallen, their leaves reaching into a storm of winters and all the rest of the seasoned, bitter and sweetness of being buried beneath their words, the longings, their terrible eyes that will not rest from what they have ever seen in Jerusalem flowers, the bloody red, the yellow stars, the gorgeous blue.

I drive on, watching the stars in the night sky travel with me. "Bethie," I call out to the strongest, brightest one, "we weren't ready. You came too early, your brilliant essence falling from somewhere, onto this turning mass, this place we called a jungle and you laughed, saying yes it was a jungle, but you liked it that way."

I continue to drive while talking into the night sky. "Even I, your closest friend, was afraid to hear you speak your mind. But you were born to survive the pain of an alien soul. Why then did you decide to die? Even though I didn't understand you, I loved you. Did you know that? You knew so much, even as a little girl, the many things you tried to teach me that only now I'm learning." *What's forbidden is so delicious, it can make you sick.* Still looking at Venus traveling with me, I call out again, "Bethie, please stay with me."

Soon picking up speed on the almost empty highway, I'm moving easily across the lanes to a faster one, continuing on with the brightest of stars while enjoying the luxury of further uninterrupted speculation.

Only the human mind in its present, perhaps still infantile state would need to decide what to remember and what to forget. Someday all our life events might be stored as pictures on discs with easy retrieval in an automatic system, and all the mental energy now required to remember them could be used instead to cope with what could never be forgotten. With such an accurate storage system, ensuring the survival of each and every moment of our lives so that nothing is ever forgotten, I wonder if forgiving would be harder or easier?

If I could click back into that whole scene between Reuben and me, would I understand more? What might a mind of the future clarify with numerical graphics of heavy arms, eyes made of numbered tears, and the measurements of red wine in glasses falling off a table? Reuben said Alex tried to hurt her, but she still wanted to play their games. Why?

Driving when tired is risky, and here I am in the fast lane. The phrase "do no harm" crosses my mind. Turning down the radio, I focus on how to make my way as safely as possible to the far right lane. If I get any more drowsy, I can quickly get off the freeway and look for a quiet street where I can park and sleep for a while.

I'm halfway home, around Oxnard. I can see the lights of the giant hotels along the freeway now, and I consider stopping at one for the night. I'm almost too tired to drive on, and it occurs to me that if I stay over somewhere, Mark will be forced to go through what I'd experienced for the past several months when he didn't come home sometimes until early in the morning. Tonight let *him* wonder. Let *him* worry and suspect. I've gone to sleep so many nights without him beside me. Now it's his turn.

Still, I keep on driving, my anger keeping me awake. Then just after going through the pass with the radio pouring love songs into the night, I hear one of the songs Mark used to sing to me, and soon I'm imagining him driving home also, feeling exhausted and lonely, trying to decide where to stop but really wanting to go home. Did he keep on driving because he knew I'd worry? Maybe he wanted me to suffer the way he did when I'd turned away from him so many nights. But what if he's home tonight and waiting for me? We might be able to talk now and, for the sake of the kids, try to be friends. Please, God, at least that.

An hour later, I come up the steep driveway to our house and click open the garage door. Soon, the light is on, and I see Mark coming toward me with outstretched arms.

"Carol, I was so worried."

"I'm okay, Mark," I call out while opening the car door. He

hurries to help me out. Then we stand there hugging, clinging with frantic affection like each other's lost child.

It's sometime after midnight. We sit in the kitchen together, finally able to talk about all the stuff that has come between us.

"Losing Bethie was more important to you than us," Mark accuses, pressing the palms of his hands against the edge of the table. "You kept pushing me away."

"I couldn't help it. I needed more time to grieve for Bethie and to find out what happened to her. I thought you would understand."

"You mean the world to me, Carol."

"As your wife? Or the kind of woman I am?"

He nods in recognition. "I'm sorry I didn't try harder to understand, but I missed your love so much."

"You held me too tight," I insist. "I had to find a way to break free."

Taking a deep breath, I continue. "And you wouldn't talk to me. What were you doing on the nights I went to the poetry readings? And what about that one weekend when you stayed in Boston?"

He looks down, averting my questioning eyes.

Now looking up again, he asks, "How about giving me... giving *us* each one secret?"

I nod quickly in agreement, letting silence release me from his now curious gaze, then feel relieved to hear him ask, "How was it with you and Reuben? Did you find out anything you didn't already know?"

"Yes. Bethie was very sick, even when she visited us, and after that. She'd undergone three operations. They left her so she couldn't have children."

"Did she care about that? I didn't think so."

"Reuben said she cared."

"What about her being with Reuben again just before she died? What was that all about?"

"I don't know. Whatever Reuben says, I'm never sure is accurate...or even makes sense. But he told me Bethie might have been abused in some way by Alex, her half-brother, so her father sent him to his uncle in France, who enrolled him in some school there, and soon after that Alex had a heart attack and died. Leona blamed Bethie and her father for his death."

"How awful! Must have been very upsetting for you to hear all that from Reuben. Do you believe him?"

"Yes, about that. I knew something was terribly wrong between Bethie and her mom, and now I know why. Talking to Reuben helped me understand more about Bethie. I think I'm more ready now to let her 'rest in peace' as my dad advised."

"He's a wise man, your dad. I've made one of the characters in my play like him." When I laugh at that, Mark says, "Hey, I like hearing you laughing. We used to have a lot of fun together. Remember?"

"I remember. Whenever I got too serious, you found ways to make me smile. The playwright in you, I guess."

"Let's have some wine," he suggests. "I saw you saved the rest of a Pinot in the fridge." He gets up and reaches in the cupboard for two wine goblets. "And let's have some toast. Does wine go with toast?"

"Why not? I'll make toast, maybe melt some cheese on it. Do

we still have cheese?"

"Unless Daniel got into it. He's our big cheese nibbler."

After we've eaten, Mark wants to talk more. To unburden himself, it seems, but I decide right then to still keep my one secret, no matter what he tells me.

"I met a woman at the Boston conference. We just talked. I didn't touch her." Though I show my surprise, he goes on bravely explaining. "I tried seeing someone once before too, but...well, nothing happened. I suppose they weren't enough like you, so I couldn't. I just wanted you."

"What was she wearing?"

"Nothing," he says, his face turning red.

I'd guessed that and want to say so, but seeing his pained look, I kiss him instead and whisper, "A wife knows best what her husband likes."

He grabs me up into his arms and carries me to bed.

TWENTY-FIVE

Molly never tells anyone about my winning the trip to Israel and giving it away. "It'll remain just between us," she promises after I've prompted, "Remember Dad always said that the highest form of charity is when you give without the person knowing who gave." She says she remembers.

"You can be part of that special righteousness, Molly," I challenge, "if you work out the details for me to give the prize ticket to Reuben for his trip home."

Molly arranges everything, and early in October, I meet Reuben at Los Angeles International to give him the ticket and see him off.

While we wait together for his flight, he expresses his appreciation. "*Toda*, Carol, thank you for your help so I can go home to Israel" His eyes seem to radiate a genuine sincerity.

Still, after we shake hands and say goodbye and he gets into the line of boarding passengers, my earlier suspicions compel me to remain standing at the departure gate until the plane takes off.

* * *

A few weeks after Reuben leaves for Israel, Seth phones to ask me to have lunch with him. The sound of his voice startles my hard-won solace. I feel my throat tighten. I take a deep breath and then refuse his invitation to lunch with a firmly stated, "Sorry, I'm tied up."

"Business," he stresses, and goes on to ask if I'll just meet at the coffee shop near his office at *The South Bay Reader,* a small press with a big voice in our community. Seth is their assistant editor.

"I can't do lunch or coffee, Seth. What's this all about?"

He then explains that he wants me to write an article detailing a program called "Poetry in the Schools." He remembers I told him about it being one of my volunteer projects for Wendy's class. "Also, I encourage you to apply for a part-time position opening at our paper soon."

"Not a good idea, Seth."

"Trust me," he reassures. "This isn't about us. I promised you that, didn't I? It won't be a problem."

"I trust you," I tell him while thinking how easy it seems for him to separate from us. I'm still wanting to hear the memory of our love somewhere in his voice.

"Okay. Then maybe not the job, but why not write the story? We'll do a big spread with pictures and some of the kids' work, and we'll pay you a hundred dollars. Is that okay with you?"

I write the story, and soon after I submit it, I'm offered the part-time job. I'm tempted, but again decide no. Maybe he can handle working beside me, but I can't.

Then Alice Williams, the editor of *The Daily News,* another local paper, calls to offer me a job. She says she's seen my story in *The South Bay Reader.* "I want to put out a weekly column on education. Would you be interested in joining our staff?"

"I'm definitely interested," I say. "Should I send you a résumé?"

"Your article and Seth Brody's recommendation are enough of a résumé for me. Just let me know soon. We want to get going on this right away."

I call back later in the week to accept her offer.

Mark thinks it's a great idea. "With the extra money, I can stop working overtime and have more time to work on my script. Thomas Tarkesian, an independent director looking for material, has expressed interest in my first draft. He even paid me three hundred bucks to bring in another draft with specified changes."

Excited and hopeful, Mark arranges a little family celebration for us at The Wooden Shoe, the children's favorite restaurant. To their delight, he orders a big stack of French fries with ketchup for starters and cherry Cokes.

While we sip wine and enjoy the children's simple sense of luxury, Mark becomes pensive. "Is this just a dream, Carol? I really never believed I'd see my play performed. I'm not in any network, you know. I just happened to tell someone at work about my play, and he knew somebody who knew somebody who knew Tarkesian."

I laugh. "I guess you're in a kind of network after all." We toast to all those somebodies who know an important somebody, and I say, "Anyway, Honey, you wrote a good play and then had the good fortune to have someone recognize it, so be happy."

"Daddy, can we order now?" Daniel asks. "We're done with our fries and I'm still hungry."

"Right on, buddy." He signals the waiter.

Mark and I are working hard to better balance our jobs with family commitments. How ironic! We've just learned how to give each other more space, but our new schedules and those of the children require prioritizing and serious co-planning on a daily basis. So tonight, when we get home, he'll check Wendy's homework and I'll see to the boys' baths and read them stories.

When I'm feeling more comfortable in my new job, I plan to get more involved in a different group, Writers Southwest. They've been trying to recruit me onto the all-volunteer editorial staff of their new monthly publication, *Southwest Passages.*

Last year a group of friends who were also writers decided to give critiques to each other and then share the costs of publishing an anthology of our best work. We put a small ad in the local paper inviting other writers to also submit their poems, stories, and articles for consideration, requesting a small reading fee to help finance it. When Writers Southwest's director, Roberto Groppa, heard about our plans, he called and suggested, "Let us take over your group's project. We're prepared to include fiction and article writing, and we'll also include our annual contest winners in the book." We agreed unanimously to accept the offer.

Then, in May, after Mark's play, *Oedipus Redux,* was performed on public television, I recommended that Writers Southwest's program committee ask him to be a guest speaker at one of their monthly meetings. With only a little coaxing on my part, he agreed.

Mark did a fine job illuminating the requirements of scriptwriting while he interwove bits of humor, all of which delighted the audience. I was so proud of him.

As part of the small honorarium Mark received, we were automatically made members of Writers Southwest, and we began attending meetings together.

Who would have guessed?

TWENTY-SIX

Rabbi Stan Wellman scheduled a program at our temple called "How To Tell Our Children About the Holocaust," and Mark and I decide to attend.

So far, like our parents, we've never spoken about the Holocaust to our children. Mark thinks it isn't necessary. "Their Sunday School teachers will do that. They know how." But I remember Bethie's basic idea that to face a horrible truth could be a psychological protection of sorts. I tell Mark about her application of that idea, the huge wall hanging in her room with the swastika that she could look at and talk about calmly while it scared me speechless.

"We should go to that talk, Mark," I persist when he is having second thoughts about attending. He takes one deep, be-patient-with-her breath and agrees to go.

After fortifying ourselves with a dinner of massive corned beef sandwiches and matzo ball soup at our local deli, we arrive a little early and choose seats two rows from the front, where a few others are seated, probably the ones who set up the coffee. We say hello and begin watching people stream in, claim seats, and soon surround the refreshment table.

"Is the coffee urn's green light on?" asks Willa Teckler, sitting next to me. Willa's son Bobby is in Daniel's class. We'd worked on one of their class art projects together. "Can't see it from here. Let's go for it," she suggests, and Mark gets up and walks back with her to see about the coffee.

I watch as they move among those waiting. Mark goes over to a trim, dark-haired man wearing jeans and a leather sport jacket. He turns toward Mark and they are shaking hands. Something about the man looks familiar, but his back is towards me, so I go for some coffee in order to meet him.

It's Seth.

"Well, hi Carol!" he says, sounding surprised.

"You know each other?" Mark asks smiling while I stare into Seth's eyes with my heart beating to the frantic voice inside me. *Show no fear.* I can hardly keep from running from the room, but somehow manage a frozen stare at Seth while answering Mark.

"Yes, we met at the poetry readings in the old jail. Remember, I used to go to them?" With effort, I ask Seth, "Are the readings there still going on?"

"Yes." He smiles at me, then looks at Mark. "Your wife is quite a poet. She read some great work to The Circle of Poets. We miss her."

Mark nods, then seems to study my face for some reaction. Does he see through this tight jaw? I feel my strength crumbling. What if later he asks? Will I be able to lie? I still hear Bethie's voice giving her character assessment of me. *You have a kind of rare moral courage.* Where did it go?

Mark asks Seth, "Is your wife here with you?

"I'm not actually married," Seth announces, his demeanor calm as always, "but my son Eddie and his mom, Delia, live with me. She isn't Jewish, so chances are I'll be the one answering his questions someday. Right now, I'm just here to report on the lecture."

I am trying to compose myself while taking all this in. *He has a son and lives with Delia. Why Not married? Maybe she's married. The free love thing. Still, I trust him. And now that he has Eddie, their love child, maybe he also needs to trust me.*

Mark says, "I guess we can use some help with how to explain the Holocaust to our kids without scaring them. It's not going to be easy."

"Let's hope Rabbi Wellman has some good ideas," I add, "but if we want more coffee, we'd better get it now. Looks like he's about to begin." Mark and Seth go for another cup while I wait for them. I can feel my heart racing again, and my face feels flushed. I try not to look at Seth while thinking that his eyes are on me.

Mark and I go back to our seats near the front left side of the room. Seth chooses a seat on the far right. When midway through the lecture, I look across the room at Seth, his eyes are on me and he's smiling the way I remember when asking while he held my face in his hands, "Are you happy, my girl for an afternoon?" and my answer, "Oh, yes, truly happy."

I look away quickly. Why is he smiling now? Is he enjoying this? I reach for Mark's hand and he moves closer and takes my hand into his while still focusing on the lecture. But I can't. I'm overwhelmed with my feelings of love for him and, at the same time, also for Seth. How is that possible? How will this all end? Even though I no longer have any desire to drive to Ojai again, here I am silently calling to Seth over the rows of heads between us, wanting to tell him I'll always remember our lovemaking that afternoon, *its unbounded knowingness and beauty, its very precious, short history like a blooming flower that fades and falls away.*

For the rest of the evening, I listen to Stan's talk in recovery mode, and when I look across the room again, I see Seth's empty chair. I guess he decided to leave before we all started saying our goodbyes and parading out to our cars.

"I'm glad we came, aren't you?" Mark asks as we climb into our beige Chevy station wagon.

"I'm not sure," I say in earnest. Then, "But I suppose Bethie had it right. She said it's important to face our fears so they don't win over us."

Mark nods and drives off.

I can hardly remember the lecture we'd come to hear, but Mark talks on about it until he notices my empty responses and says, "You worry too much, Carol. The kids are still young. We have more time to deal with this."

I wish I could stop worrying so much about Mark and our children and not think about Seth anymore, but that's impossible. What if I keep running into Seth with Eddie, his little boy, when he brings him to our temple preschool? I may someday even meet Delia. What does she know? Will she say something to someone we know, who then tells Mark?

"We'll work this out when we need to, Carol," he says, and my heart jumps into my throat until he adds, "We'll find a way to gradually tell the kids, like our parents did. Actually, wasn't that what Rabbi was saying? Only one guy in the audience disagreed."

"I agreed with Rabbi Stan," I answer, relieved to be breathing normally again. "Bethie said that one day her parents told her all about the horrors, the ovens, everything when she was only nine years old, and she had nightmares after that for the longest time."

We turn down our street and Mark pulls into our driveway. He turns off the engine and, facing me, asks in a stiff, guarded tone, "That reporter...what was his name? Seth Brody. How well do you know him?"

My heart is racing but slows enough for me to breathe when I answer, "Not really well." *True, I don't really know him anymore. He found another girl for an afternoon....* "I know him from The Circle of Poets' meetings and from his work."

"You poets are really strange," Mark declares.

"I suppose."

If Mark knows, he'll ask again, want me to say more, and if I tell him my one secret, nothing will ever be the same between us.

You have what Tillich calls rare moral courage.

Well, maybe so, Bethie, but I didn't offer up my secret and Mark did, and I'm not even sure what I'd say if he were to ask more questions about Seth and me.

✳ ✳ ✳

The house is very quiet. Even with the bedroom window open, only a few cars make their familiar sounds on our street. I get into bed after taking a sleeping pill to help me rest from the ordeal earlier of seeing Seth again and having Mark meet him, and then learning about Delia and Eddie, their love child. I reach for my comforting pillow, hoping to try meditating to a calmer place, but that upsetting scene at the temple merges with the discussion about finding the right time and way to tell our Jewish children they belong to the survivors of the six million non-survivors of historical hatred, abuse, and murder… and now, all of this suddenly quieting… fading into the moonlight seen through the curtains waving beside me as I sense myself falling a little deeper…

Mark is with me, moving closer, and then his strong hand tugs at my waist. "Carol," he murmurs, "tell me about you and that guy, Seth. Did you sleep with him?" The cold shock of his words run through me, and I know I must speak to stop their pain. "Yes," I tell him. "Just once." His hand stiffens against me, and I cry out, "I loved you both then, but I chose you, Mark. I love you…love…"

I sit up gasping for breath, then feel relieved when I hear Mark in the shower. Only a dream, but Jenna would say it must be telling me something. Maybe to prepare for what I fear most?

TWENTY-SEVEN

J enna writes that she is coming to Los Angeles to show her port-
folio of new paintings at an art studio somewhere in Westwood.
She asks if I can pick her up at LAX. We can go to the gallery first
together, I'm thinking, and then have lunch nearby before I drop
her back at the airport. I call her to say yes and ask if she'd like to
stay over. "Oh, I'd love to, she says, "but I can't."

I see Jenna now in front of the United Airlines terminal. She's
wearing a long, multi-colored skirt, beige sweater, a thick brown
leather belt, and matching boots. I wave, smiling to see how wonderful she looks, and motion her in. She's carrying a large, flat
black bag on her shoulder with, I suppose, her paintings, and I'm
excited to soon be able to see them.

She hops in the car, and we reach for each other with hugs and
kisses. Then I make my way out with the long trail of airport cars
going north on Sepulveda while she fills me in on her life since
she'd left for Michigan and moved in with her parents.

"My agent connected me with this little art gallery in
Westwood we're going to, and they sold one of my paintings,
Carol. I wanted you to see it before it's going to be picked up

tomorrow. And I have so much to tell. A lot has happened since we talked before I left."

"Deb and Mindy must be so big now, Jenna. How are they doing?"

"They're fine, I guess, but sometimes they're sad because they don't see their dad very often. Just on Christmas morning when he and his current partner stay overnight at a hotel nearby and come with presents for them. I always invite them both to stay for dinner, but they never do, just say they're working and have a flight going out soon. Mindy used to cry when John left, but not anymore since… well, guess what?"

"Tell me!"

"I'm seeing someone, Carol, and my kids like him a lot. I met him after I graduated from Michigan State and started teaching at Lansing High. Hank teaches math there, and it wasn't long before we started dating."

"Sounds promising, Jenna. What's he like?"

"Well, he's a tall, dark, and still handsome forty-year-old guy, smart and good with kids. A great teacher!"

"Divorced too, like you?"

"No. Hank's never been married. He says he's only slept around, but he's now totally focused on me, and I love that about him."

Slept around. I immediately think of Bethie, but I let go of mentioning my concerns. Jenna's a big girl, and so level-headed.

"Anyway," Jenna continues, "I told him about John, and Hank insisted that I get tested for AIDS before we sleep together, and I'm glad about that because I never thought to do that. I should have. We both got tested."

After I let Jenna off in front of Artworks West Gallery, I begin looking for parking. No small task. I give up and drive into a parking lot a few blocks away.

Walking back to the gallery, I feel so happy for Jenna. Her life seems to be working out well now.

When I enter the studio, I see Jenna standing in front of a large canvas on the wall in front of her, and she beckons me to her side. She looks worried. Why, I wonder.

Now pointing to the canvas, she asks, "What do you think of this?" My mouth falls open in surprise.

"Jenna, it's… it's my dream scene in the garage with Wendy and the cat, isn't it?"

"Yes. Did I capture how you described it to me?"

"It looks exactly…" I take a deep breath. "Jenna, it's exactly like my dream. Just looking at it gives me the same scary feeling as when I woke up. It's like I'm back in the garage with Wendy and that horrible cat!"

"I tried hard to paint what you described."

"Well, you did that… except you've painted a lot more shelving and tools than we've ever had."

"Artistic license," she says and we both laugh.

"There's Wendy in her bedclothes," I point out, "and the empty pitcher she's holding while the black cat is drinking from the bowl at her feet. But who's that pretty woman standing so stiff and scared in the background wearing my blue coat? Artistic license, I guess."

"Of course it's you," Jenna says. "And since she was about to be attacked by that cat, I painted its wild eyes green and black, and its scruffy coat to foreshadow the approaching danger." She holds the tag up to me and I read: The Milk of Kindness, Beware! $500.

On our way back to the airport, Jenna asks, "Are you really okay with me painting your dream and then selling it for five hundred dollars?"

"Of course. You're an artist, Jenna. Besides, I really wouldn't want that nightmare hanging in my house."

"I didn't think so. But is it still upsetting you?"

"Only sometimes. I'm still trying to figure out who in my dream might be the cat that attacked me."

"Well keep trying, and someday maybe you will."

"And even if that happens, Jenna, then what?"

"Then at least you can avoid trying to feed it."

As I move slowly through the heavy traffic toward the airport, we continue enjoying the little time we have left and plan a future get-together with the children.

TWENTY-EIGHT

Nobody in their right mind would visit Arizona in the summer, but in June, I decide to forgo sanity and drive to Tucson to visit my parents for the first time since their move from our ranch-style family home to an assisted-living community. During that same weekend, I plan to attend the twentieth reunion of my high school class. The boys are at camp, and Mark says he's looking forward to spending a quiet weekend at home rather than join me and endure the 120 degrees forecasted, but I figure I'll always be in air-conditioning from car to hotel to my parents' place, then to the reunion.

Still, I'm experienced enough to be packing sunscreen lotions and two hats, in case I dangerously lose one, and a pair of thick gloves so I can touch the steering wheel after returning to the car each time. If I leave Thursday and stay overnight in Phoenix, I'll arrive in Tucson early in the morning when the heat is not as oppressive.

* * *

While checking in at the Phoenix Thunderbird, I recall the last time I was here years ago with my parents on our way to visit Dad's older brother, Uncle Ben, in Sedona during a rainstorm.

We stayed here that night listening to the rain and thunder and eating fried chicken from the bucket that Mom sent Dad out to pick up for dinner. I can still see us sitting at the ends of the two double beds, parts of chicken in our hands and napkins on our laps, and Mom saying it's okay to eat fried chicken with our hands, but Dad responding, "Only in America," and then insisting we at least say a prayer of thanks over the buttermilk biscuits that Molly and I loved.

After my long trip today from Irvine to Phoenix with only a stop in Blythe, I'm exhausted. I treat myself to room service and order the pricey hamburger plate with fries. When it arrives, I can relax and eat, then shower before going to bed with some TV movie. It hardly matters which one since I'm hoping it'll put me to sleep.

As planned, I leave Phoenix very early in the morning to go on to Tucson, where my first stop is an early check-in at the Sunrise Inn. I leave my bags and ask for a map of the city. Then I'm off again, wrestling the hot car with my gloves on to find a supermarket where I can buy something to bring my parents.

Luckily there's one nearby that's bound to feel even too cool in contrast to outside. It'll be a great relief.

I make it into the market, and while looking for the bakery section, I walk past the garden section and eye the gorgeous bunches of dazzling colored flowers. Then I notice a few bouquets of long-stem white roses, which immediately remind me of the ones I wanted to put on Bethie's grave. I could really do that during this trip. I'll buy them before I leave in the morning and use my city map to find Greenacre Cemetery, where Bethie is buried.

With that plan in mind, I head over to the bakery department, choose a container of apricot rugulach, Dad's favorite pastries, and then proceed to the check-out counter. It's still early enough for service without having to stand in a line.

With the help of my map and a few well-placed signs, I locate the visitor parking area and, after some further directions in the main lobby of the Shalom Campus-of-Care, I find my parents' apartment on the third floor of the west wing, at the end of a hallway flanked on both sides by extra-wide doors in order to accommodate wheelchairs. Having phoned earlier to say I'm coming, I soon learn they've been ready and waiting for a long time. My first knock brings Dad immediately to open the door and greet me with a strong hug. Mom, in the background, is wiping her hands on a towel. Then she comes forward, arms outstretched. Our hug, as always loose and awkward, is followed by our half-smiles.

As soon as I enter the combined living room and kitchen of their small, one-bedroom apartment, the sad reality of how much they have given up to make their lives easier is obvious.

They show me around, cheerfully pointing out the few familiar pieces of furniture they've managed to squeeze into two small rooms. "Even our old maple kitchen table," Dad says. Their new walls, covered with many old photos of our family, announce how much the past has become an almost overwhelming presence. *Something about that table...*

Mom makes tea, and we sit together at the little maple table in the kitchen off the living room while Dad reviews the decisions required for such a move. "We brought our best things that would fit."

The maple table… a troubling memory… fading in and out.

"You made it nice," I offer.

"We like our new home," Mom declares. "And we have good friends here, don't we, Aaron?" Dad doesn't answer her. I wonder if he's having a harder time adjusting here.

"And we have our own parking space out in front," Mom says.

"Yes," Dad adds, "and they also have a nice bus for group trips. We went to an art museum last week."

"Have some cake, Carol," Mom says, "your favorite. I baked it special for you." She cuts us each a piece of her prize-winning chocolate marble cake, and I happily indulge.

Before we finish the first slice, Mom offers us another. Dad gives his usual "enough is enough" hand sign and stands up. "Carol, you'll excuse me. I promised to help Bob-down-the-hall fine tune his television set. He says he gets too much red."

Dad leaves then, tool kit in hand, and Mom pours more tea.

"You know, Carol," she begins, "your Wendy looks so lovely here in her high school picture she just sent me." She points to it among several others on their refrigerator door and then to the one yellowing with age. "And look, here's one of your school pictures I found when we were packing." She holds it out.

"Wendy looks like you, don't you think? You were such a pretty little girl." *The cat… I could never make Mom happy.*

My lips freeze in a half-smile as her revised view of me stabs at my heart. I count to ten twice, my method invented long ago to fight back tears, but it isn't working this time. My eyes flood and Mom notices.

"Carol, what's wrong, dear?"

All those years of longing to hear the words she's saying so easily now. Has her whole being somehow mellowed in the short time she's been here in her new home? I blot my eyes with a table napkin while answering, "I'm just so glad to see you and Dad so... happy here."

She smiles. "We're doing okay, Carol." She pats my hand. Then, her forehead suddenly wrinkles in obvious distress, and she asks, "How's your sister? Not pregnant yet, I suppose."

"I don't think so. Anyway, she's fine, Mom."

"Fine? Not to have a child?"

"Well, kids do cost a lot to raise," I offer, hoping to lighten the conversation. "Molly and Bob travel a lot now, but whenever they're in town, they love to entertain our kids...take them to Disneyland, bring them gifts."

Mom frowns and changes the subject to Grandma's cups, describing how she'd packed them very carefully to bring to her new cupboard. We continue drinking our tea in them and nibble at our cake.

"God works in strange ways," she muses while refilling Grandma's cups and passing me the sugar bowl.

"What do you mean?" I'm guessing she's waited for me to decide to ask.

"I'm remembering when you were born. I only wanted a boy...a son for Aaron."

I bite my lip and close my eyes, but she goes on with what she perceives as some kind of wisdom she wants to share. "I already had a girl, my beautiful Molly."

I don't like sugar in tea, but with trembling hands, I pour several spoonfuls into my cup while she continues, "But you gave me grandchildren, not Molly." She rattles her cup in its saucer. "I'm sure Molly wants a baby, but Bob doesn't, she says." Her cup rattles again. "It's not natural, Molly, I tell her, and it's selfish, but she doesn't listen."

"So, what does God's work have to do with all this?"

"So…in the end, I'm grateful to Him now that he gave me you." Smiling again, she adds, "You brought me three fine grandchildren."

Nausea, my longtime coping skill, sweeps over me. I stand up quickly and run to the bathroom sink to let my anger explode. Then I splash my face again and again while hearing Bethie's voice urging me to get control of myself.

Don't let her mess with you!

Meanwhile, my grateful-to-God mother is standing at the door of the bathroom waiting, not realizing how close she's come to being in harm's way, and she asks, "Are you sick, Carol?" Then, with a faint note of joy in her voice, "Maybe you're pregnant with another blessing?"

One, two, three…

I leave the bathroom and, still struggling to appear sane, I sit back down at the table across from her and sense the words I've controlled for so long now crawling forward as if on their own power, and like nothing else matters, my child voice cracks through my tears and asks her, "Why didn't you love me?"

Looking surprised, she pushes back in her chair, her tearful eyes seeming to ask me why I'm spoiling my visit.

"I tried," she finally utters.

"Tried?"

"You were named for Caroline. For *her*."

"I know that. She was Dad's sister. He loved her."

"Yes. Caroline always looked down on me, always criticizing, laughing at me. Always so mean, but your father protected her when they escaped from Europe, and she lived with us until she died just before you were born. He and Grandma wanted you to have her name, so..." She reaches over and touches my hand. "So you," she mumbles with bitterness, "you reminded me of her."

She pulls her hand away, sits back in her chair and tries to drink her cold tea, but her hand is trembling. She puts the cup down and grabs my hand. "I'm sorry. I wanted to do better, but..."

Dad opens the front door just then and comes in announcing in a loud flourish the success of his neighborly endeavor. "His TV looks perfect now. Just a little turn on a knob, all it needed." He sits down next to me and asks, "Why the long face, Carol?"

Mom answers quickly for me. "She's fine. She's glad to see us settled and happy here." When she turns and looks at me for agreement, I read fear in her eyes for the first time and cover her hand with mine.

"I'm fine, Dad," I say, and Mom, looking relieved, gives me a half-smile and stands up to clear the table. Dad lets his question drop with a skeptical look.

Anxious to leave now, I stand up to say goodbye.

"So soon you're going?" he asks.

"I really should. This evening I plan to attend my high school class reunion at La Mesa High. I need to get back to the hotel to get ready."

He walks me to the door. "Next time stay longer."

"Yes, I will. Molly said our favorite English teacher, Miss D, turned up at her reunion two years ago. I'm hoping to see her too."

"That would be nice," Mom says over her shoulder while standing at the sink washing the tea-stained cups.

"Come again soon," Dad murmurs, kissing my cheek.

"Bye, Mom," I call out. She waves without turning.

Before getting into the elevator, I look back at the end of the hall and see that Dad is still standing at the door. He waves, and I throw him a kiss.

While driving to the hotel, I'm thinking about the enormous power parents have to give and withhold love. Maybe that knowledge is too overwhelming to realize within the confines of daily family life. In any case, my mother didn't seem to have a clue.

At the next red light ahead, when I slow to a stop and wait, the faintly-recalled kitchen scene returns, but this time it invades my mind like a dark cloud coming before a terrible storm, and Molly and I are at the center of its possibly destructive power.

When I find a parking space at the hotel, I sit in my car for a while and let myself cry until the dark cloud clears, and then I see and remember.

* * *

I'm there with Molly at our maple kitchen table.

We hear Mommy shouting at Daddy, "She has to go. I don't want her here anymore." I'm afraid she means me. I start to cry and lean over on Molly's arm.

"She has to leave," Molly whispers.

"Who?"

"Grandma. Mom doesn't like her."

"Why?"

"I don't know. Maybe because she speaks Russian with Daddy sometimes so Mommy can't understand."

They come into the kitchen, still arguing, and Daddy is carrying two suitcases and wearing a hat and coat.

"Where do you think you're going?" Mommy asks in a funny, wobbling voice like mine is when I'm afraid.

"I'm taking Ma to Ben's in Arizona. We'll stay there, where she's welcome," Daddy says in his troubled voice.

"No," Mommy screams, and she grabs the suitcase that's a little broken on one side and throws it across the kitchen floor. It opens in front of us, scattering our grandma's underclothes and flowered dresses everywhere, along with the white lace hat and the pearls she wears on Saturdays.

When Molly gasps and starts to cry, I know what's happening must be very bad, so I cry too while we watch Daddy pick up Grandma's clothes and put them back in the suitcase, now more broken. Then he comes over to us looking very sad and kisses us, and then he walks out the door.

"Why are you two crying?" Mommy's angriest voice asks us. "He'll be back."

"No," Molly tells her, "He won't come back without Grandma."

Mommy leaves the kitchen and we run to the window and see Grandma sitting in Daddy's truck. "Where are they going?" I ask Molly.

"To Uncle Ben's, far away." She's crying again. "We won't have a father, or see Grandma anymore."

Mommy returns to the kitchen and hugs Molly. "Stop crying. Go wash your face and I'll braid your hair. It's time to go to school, my first-grade girl."

Molly shakes her head no and keeps on crying.

"You heard me, Molly. Stop the tears. He'll be back soon, I said. Go now! I'm getting ready to spank you."

Molly stamps out of the kitchen while I tell Mommy, like Molly, "He won't come back without Grandma."

Mommy's angry face comes closer to mine. "Shut your mouth, Carol, or you'll get something you won't like!"

I look down into my bowl and throw up all my cereal.

"Take that mess to the sink," she shouts, "then go change your dress. I'm not taking you to nursery school today smelling like that!"

In the bedroom, I tear all the buttons off the front of my smelly dress and throw it under the bed.

When Mommy comes for me, she sees another pile of vomit on the bed. "Stay here in this stinking room today."

It seems a long time until Daddy comes home with Grandma. He brings in her new suitcase, and Mommy smiles at him, then goes upstairs with Grandma to help her unpack.

* * *

Sitting in my car now after reliving the trauma of that terrible morning, I'm feeling a little sick, but I don't need to vomit. I'm able to compose myself enough to enter the hotel lobby and take the elevator to my room.

Soon I start to prepare for this evening's reunion event, which is a "social" to be held in the La Mesa High auditorium. I shower and slip into my sleeveless black dress and black, low heeled shoes. Then, hesitating for only a moment, I put on the earrings I wore when I went to be with Seth. I want to look as young as I can now. Probably everyone else coming feels the same way.

I wonder who'll remember me after twenty years. It always seemed that Bethie and I were hardly noticed, walking around together in our own little world. Anyway, if Miss D. comes, even if she doesn't recognize me, I'm sure I'll know her, and I plan to tell her how much I loved her creative writing class and that she has always been my favorite teacher.

TWENTY-NINE

After two uncomfortable hours at my high school class reunion, seeing faded smiles with familiar voices, I'm now realizing that my favorite teacher is probably not coming. *Miss D, when you left us suddenly that year, where did you go? Flying free, our friend, our butterfly, did you break a wing, fall into the sea? Where?*

Disappointed, I decide to leave, when a man, looking to be in his late thirties like us, approaches me. He seems very self-confident in his navy suit and red tie.

"Hi. I'm Raymond Mulbert," he says, extending his hand. "You're Carol Mandell, right?" I don't recognize him or his name, but shake hands and force a smile.

"Right. I'm Carol Mandell Simon. How nice that you remember me."

"I'll confess. The lady in the pink sweater over there pointed you out. I'm a feature writer for *New Science Review*." He hands me his card. "I'm working on a story about someone who graduated with your class in '64. Elizabeth Hartung?"

"I see." I swallow hard. Hearing Bethie's name always brings a flood of mixed feelings.

"Well, nice meeting you, Mr. Mulbert, but I'm just on my way out. I've got a long trip from Tucson back to California." I start walking toward the door.

He follows me, saying, "Can I talk to you for a few minutes? I've come a long way and I'd really appreciate it."

I stop and face him. "Why me?"

He points to a table nearby. "Please. It won't take long." Annoyed now at being delayed, I go over to the table with him but continue to stand, planning to leave as soon as I can.

"I'm writing a feature on Language Trees, an approach to linguistic evolution. I was told by one of your classmates that you were a close friend of a girl everyone called Bethie, who was Dr. Elizabeth Hartung, a professor at University of New Mexico."

"Yes, we were best friends in high school and then at the University of Chicago. She died many years ago. I can't imagine anyone wanting... I mean, why a story now?"

"I know it seems after-the-fact. Everyone I've spoken to in linguistic and anthropological research mentions her suicide and the loss of such a promising young scholar. The word out now is that her theory, published in her dissertation and considered then as off-the-wall, was right on." He sits down and slides his fingers through the thick strands of black hair falling across his forehead. Pushing them back, he takes a pen and notebook out of his briefcase. I take the chair next to him, anxious to know what he's heard about Bethie's dissertation. She'd never told me anything about it.

Mulbert says, "According to Dr. Morgan, a linguistics professor at the University of Chicago, there's a transference of words or phrases in languages between generations, which Dr. Hartung theorized as having a network effect rather than a tree effect, more synergistic. She'd also mentioned the possibility of actual brain activities related to specific parts of words. Very original for its time and now the current thinking on that subject." He pulls a pipe out of his jacket pocket, lights it, and continues.

"Dr. Morgan recalled Dr. Hartung saying she wrote detailed notes along with the original copy of her dissertation in some other language--Hebrew, I think he said. Morgan felt certain that if she were alive now, she'd be receiving The Bridgefield, a prestigious science award with a large monetary prize."

"I'm not surprised. She was brilliant...a genius, in fact. Our teachers all knew that. We all did. But girls aren't supposed to be geniuses. Not then anyway."

"Right." He smiles weakly while jotting something in his notebook. "I plan to include that angle also."

Angle? I can see where this is leading. Mulbert obviously already knew the basic facts about Bethie's life. He's searching for more details about what must have been the professional gossip at the time. How depressing to think that if Bethie were still alive, she would probably feel gratified by some current scholarly recognition. Now it's too late.

I slide my arms into my coat sleeves and stand up, then say in my sharpest voice, "How nice that she'll be appreciated after she's dead!"

Not to be hindered by my anger, Mulbert presses on with, "Can you tell me more about her? I want to let people know her not only as a woman scientist and scholar, but also as your friend. That lady over there in the pink sweater said you knew her better than anyone."

"I'm not sure about that."

"Do you remember some of her main interests during your high school years together?"

"Bethie was interested in everything."

"Did she belong to any clubs?"

"She played in the orchestra." I smile now recalling to myself the picture of Bethie sitting in the last row of the violin section, trying to play only on middle C whenever it came up in the violin parts. She didn't know how to play, she had admitted only to me, but she thought she might need more extracurricular credits for her scholarship applications. I can still see her holding her violin just right and looking so confident. She must have practiced how to do all that and how to read notes instead of practicing how to play the songs.

Mulbert, noticing my smile, joins with, "I'll bet she was good, huh?"

"Without even trying," I laugh.

"Was she popular with the guys?"

"What do you mean?" I tease, knowing what he has in mind. "How should I know?"

His face flushes, but he continues to probe, like any good reporter, first asking simple questions, hoping to put me more at ease, then moving into the more difficult areas of his search while I avoid giving him information.

Finally, becoming impatient, he blurts out what, in fact, he'd really come to discover. "Why would a woman like her end her life at the pinnacle of her career? I've been told by more than a few of her colleagues that she was sort of strange, some thought promiscuous, even by modern standards. Was she?"

My disgust with where his questions are going now mixes with my bitterness over Bethie's belated fame, and I tell him, "I don't want to do this." I turn away and start to leave, taking a few steps toward the door.

Mulbert jumps up and follows me, calling out, "I'll pay for your time." He keeps pace as I rush out through the open lobby doors of the auditorium, and he continues pursuing me with the darts of my own inner questions.

"Did you actually believe that it could have been suicide? Wasn't she, in fact, sick then? She was a tenured professor. Why would she kill herself with all she had going for her?"

"Still not interested," I call back while quickening my pace to the parking lot.

Soon I hear his desperate voice calling over a row of cars, "If you change your mind, you can reach me anytime at the magazine."

THIRTY

Greenacres Memorial Park, as it's called, is a very beautiful cemetery with numerous trees offering shade to visiting loved ones and banks of burning flowers. Leaving my car windows open, I walk along the paths of graves with my wide-brimmed hat on and sunglassses barely shielding me from the angry rays of the sun until I finally locate Bethie's gravestone. Beside it, a young tree has already begun to drop its hot, dried leaves, spreading a coat of many colors over her grave.

I lay the bouquet of white roses I'd purchased earlier among the dried orange and bronze leaves around her stone, which reads simply:

ELIZABETH HARTUNG (1948-1974).

Here, as in graveyards all over the world, many others must come like me with so much left unsaid, and wishing for a second chance to release the painful words unspoken in hopes of finding a new peace.

I spread the towel I brought from the hotel over the hot stone bench and sit down. My plan is to sit here between Bethie's and the neighboring grave for as long as I'm able to endure the rising temperature and let my mind's heart listen to our silent dialogue.

"Bethie, I'm here."

I've been waiting for you.

Though her answering comes from within myself, it feels natural to hear her voice as close to me as breathing, her spirit and her story so interwoven with mine and what I chose to remember in order to make sense of our lives and our friendship.

"The last time we were together, we'd both changed so much. You were still a free spirit but also a woman of the world while I'd chosen the life of a married woman and mother of three, working at home. You seemed so disappointed in me, and that hurt, so I said the words that made you feel unwelcome and you left.

Carol, why didn't you tell me the way you felt about what I said?

"As always, I used silence to freeze over the pain so it wouldn't show I cared."

Do you forgive me?

"Yes, immediately after you left. Still, I didn't call or write, and when you got sick, I didn't even know. Please forgive me for not asking you to stay and talk."

I forgive you, I hear her whisper into the leaves waving their golden colors in the hot wind that's gathering them everywhere around my feet.

Even in this shady spot, the flowers I'd brought only a few minutes ago have wilted, and more of the heat promised for the day is rising steadily, reminding me with the start of a headache that I must soon leave.

While more and more leaves surrender and fall on Bethie's grave and the parched gray grass around me, I still want to stay here with Bethie as long as I can, bring us to the solace of

saying the words not spoken that might have changed everything... I want to go back to the time before I encouraged her
to leave, before the time when Van Gogh said that friends are
turned into murderers.

"Bethie, I know how sad you were about your brother's death."

Nothing is pure, Carol, not even sadness.

"I've finally learned that."

I always knew.

"Even when you were a little girl?"

*My father and Alex never got along. I guess because Dad obviously
favored me. But Alex and I loved each other, even though he sometimes said
he wanted to hurt me. But he never did. So that day when he said we had
to stop playing our pretending game, I didn't understand why.*

"You never told me about that."

You never seemed to want to talk to me about love.

"Silence wasn't always my friend, Bethie. But you realized that
too, didn't you?"

*Yes. I remember that day when we sat together on the steps of La Mesa
High's auditorium, I tried.*

"Still, we had some good times together, didn't we?"

*We did. You were still my very special friend. I loved you and wanted
to tell you that.*

"At La Mesa High that morning, I knew."

It occurs to me that this is the closest I've come to understanding the benefits of something like a Catholic confession. Somehow,
my feelings of guilt and regret are weighing less heavily now, and I
want to talk more with Bethie, but it's getting hotter each minute,

and if I don't leave very soon, I could faint here beside her grave with no one in sight to help."I have to go now," I tell her, "but I'll come back in the spring. I promise."

I'll be waiting.

Before leaving, I whisper my last cinquain to her.

"I dream
Of you reborn
full of a new spring's sound,
seeded and nursed, all leaves returned
to me."

THIRTY-ONE

Arriving back in Phoenix a few hours later, I check into the Thunderbird again, change into a comfortable, sleeveless dress, then brave the ninety degrees of heat to walk to the Mexican restaurant across the street just after sunset, when the sky is streaked with a wide band of pink, yellow, and shades of orange-red, and the temperature has dropped fifteen degrees, which seems like a kind relief.

I order a taco salad and coffee, and after enjoying my meal, sit for a long time over a second cup of coffee to review the events of the day: My visit to my parents in their tiny apartment, where I came to better understand the irony of my mother's abuse of me as solace for her own pain. Then, at the reunion, Mulbert finding me and describing Bethie's award-winning thesis while continuing to pump me for very personal information about Bethie, along with his wild speculation that she might have been murdered.

Did helping Bethie kill herself actually make Reuben a murderer? If so, I helped him escape. What then am I? *I'm never going to grow old. I'll know when...* Of course, her choice. Still, according to Van Gogh....

Back at the hotel, I'm glad that my room for tonight is the same one I had before. I'm hoping the added comfort of this familiarity will bring me a good night's sleep. I climb into bed and try to read some of the brochures handed out at the reunion. Maybe they're boring enough to help me drift off.

An hour later, I'm still lying here wide awake. I keep thinking about Bethie's death, which now has become an endless dialogue with the awesome responsibility we shared in each other's lives. So much to remember, so much I hadn't understood-- the mysteries inside our complicated friendship, the long silences between us, and then, after she died, how her story became *our* story, Bethie's and mine.

When I close my eyes, everything Reuben told me in Santa Barbara invades. *Carol, you were the one she loved most. I played her games like Alex. Whatever she wanted. Many others. Three operations. So much pain. She wanted children. I helped her get more pills. I did what she wanted.*

Still unable to fall asleep, I go over Reuben's plan to bring Bethie's original notes and a copy of her thesis to Professor Micah Stern at Hebrew University in Jerusalem. That's what Reuben said Bethie wanted. Was that why she'd asked for his help? Did she believe he would go back to Israel at her request with the money she'd left him, and bring the original copy of her thesis to Stern? He'd said he wasn't sure he would have enough money for the plane ticket. He said he always did whatever she wanted. But now, on his own in Jerusalem, would he?

* * *

I arrive home exhausted, but I immediately call and leave a message on Mulbert's phone: "This is Carol Simon. I know the whereabouts of a copy of Dr. Elizabeth Hartung's original thesis and her notes, and I want to help you write your story. She was an amazing woman and, even if only now, deserves the recognition you mentioned for her original work. If you're interested in that kind of information, please return my call. My number is..."

Afterward, I dial the long string of international numbers that will connect me to Jerusalem.

Discussion Questions

1. Does the title reflect Bethie and Carol's friendship at various crossroads?

2. Who is the narration mostly about?

3. Both women had parents who were children of survivors; would you consider them to be survivors also?

4. How did Bethie's name changing as a child affect her?

5. What was Carol's greatest challenge beyond the loss of her closest friend?

6. Did Carol's relationship with her mother ever change?

7. Discuss the contrasting friendships between Carol and Bethie and between Carol and Jenna. How did these relationships change?

8. Do you think Carol's inner dialogue in the cemetery scene will help her to move on?

9. Like Van Gogh, do you consider either Reuben or Carol to be murderers?

10. What do you think contributed most to Bethie's decision to end her life?

Acknowledgements

I am grateful first to the TLC WRITERS group for their insightful critiques during those years I spent drafting this novel.

Thanks to Marcia Spiegel for including me in her women's poetry project and the Creative Jewish Women's Alliance.

Very heartfelt thanks to my daughter, Gwen, for her sensitive, literary advice and for recommending her friend, Rivka Levin, to assist me; my appreciation and love go to them both.

I'm also thankful for the opportunity to share the many different perspectives of those in my Temple Menorah book group and my women's monthly book group at Ruth Reisman's.

To my favorite hairdresser, Shawnie Vargas, my special thanks for her friendship and her photo of me on the back cover.

Also, I want to thank both my publishing consultant, Tina, and author representative, Justene, for their kind guidance.

Finally, with appreciation for his patience, insights and amazing copyediting skills, my admiration and love go to my grandson, Troy Schubert.

CPSIA information can be obtained at www.ICGtesting.com
Printed in the USA
BVOW05s0843150914

366835BV00001B/72/P